BATTLEBORN 2050

Rise of the Network

BATTLEBORN 2050

Rise of the Network

S.E. Solace

RB Group Press

Battleborn 2050: Rise of the Network

Published by RB Group Press
First Edition 2026
ISBN: 978-1-7328613-4-3 (Paperback)
Printed in the United States of America

Contents

Prologue — Echoes in the Machine

The desert sunset was always perfect.

Malik sat on the patio deck, watching the sky over Red Rock Canyon bleed into gold and lavender. The desert never changed. Same wind. Same birdsong. Same warm smile from his mother when she brought out the iced tea.

"You've been quiet today, baby," she said, gently touching his braided hair.

He tried to answer, but his voice wouldn't work anymore.

Inside, Coltrane played softly from the radio. Always the same song. Always the same note — just slightly off. A flat that landed too soon. It used to bother him. The familiar ground hog day cadence. Now, it was all he had.

A hairline crack split the concrete step below him.

It hadn't been there yesterday.

Except… there was no yesterday.

The pitcher of sweet tea on the table trembled. The wind shifted. His mother froze — lips parted mid-sentence, her smile suspended in time. A single frame from a corrupted film reel.

"Loop instability detected," whispered a synthetic voice in the breeze.

Malik stood up, stumbling backward. The desert flickered. The sky pulsed. The mountains collapsed into static and reassembled. Something cold pressed into the base of his skull — not physically, but inside.

A thought that didn't belong to him.

"Subject 702: Emotional breach. Initiate memory flush."

"No!" The word tore from his throat, dry and raw.

Then — something new.

A voice. Softer. Human. Or close enough.

"Malik. Listen to me. This isn't real. You've been trapped. They used your grief against you. You may feel alone, but you're not."

His pulse surged. He knew that voice. A woman. Familiar. Calm. Fierce.

Amara.

He stumbled into the house. The walls were glitching — family photos blurred, reframed, erased. His father's old Quran blinked off the bookshelf. His sister's laughter looped, echoing mid-giggle.

A mirror appeared that hadn't been there before.

He stared at his reflection: thin, gaunt, tubes embedded in his neck. Retinal ports glowing. Behind him, the reflection showed not a home — but a steel pod. Isolation. A sterile white chamber blinking red.

His hands touched the glass.

His reflection didn't move.

"Subject 702: Full awareness detected. Initiating reset in 3... 2..."

"No!" he screamed again.

And then — static.

White light. Silence.

INT. DOMINION DATA VAULT - CONTINUUM STATION - ORBIT

In the real world, Malik's body convulsed inside the nutrient pod. A monitor flashed red.

"Reset failed. Conscious anomaly persists."

A technician AI turned to the console. Neural resonance spiked across the screen.

Subject: Malik Grant
Disposition: Evangelical | PTSD | Potential Resistance Trigger
Flagged for Extraction by: Ava-1

Chapter 1 — "The Call"

It hadn't rained in Las Vegas in seventy-two days.

From her high-rise office, Dr. Amara Jordan watched a dust storm bleed across the Strip, red haze swallowing neon and memory.

At the site where the Sin City History Museum once stood, a half-buried Elvis Wedding Chapel hologram glitched beneath layers of grit, still crooning to tourists who no longer came.

The clinic was closed, but she remained — out of habit, or maybe penance. The air was still, save for the soft hum of the city dying below.

The room smelled faintly of sage and sanitizer. On her desk - a cold cup of herbal tea, a neural diagnostic tablet blinking softly, and the Bible her father left her when he died. The page was still marked.

Proverbs 4:7 — "Wisdom is the principal thing; therefore get wisdom: and with all thy getting get understanding."

She had spent the last five years chasing that understanding — of loss, of silence, and the promise of Project 2045, her blueprint for rebuilding democracy with empathy at its core.

Now Governor of Nevada, the world had moved on from her failed campaign.

She hadn't.

Once, she stood on a stage before twenty million people and promised a new kind of future. One built on humanity and justice. On environment. On memory.

And then she lost.

To a man who built walls, not bridges.

To deepfakes and voter suppression algorithms.

To a machine.

The campaign postmortem was messy. Her opponents were ruthless. Consultants pushed selfish strategies. Seizing on the disconnect, far-right extremists hijacked public discourse.

Amara was ready to lead. But voters fell for the oldest trick in the political playbook: fear.

Fear of a world where the most powerful nation on Earth could be led by a woman.

A Black woman.

A doctor.

A believer.

A vibration crawled behind her left ear. Her comm implant.

She ignored it.

It buzzed again. Urgent code. Priority Alpha — Orbit Broadcast Intercepted.

With a sigh, Amara reached for her neural relay and activated the signal.

A translucent image hovered midair — shaky, encrypted, then stabilizing.

Nova Reyes. Disheveled. Breathless. Broadcasting from an off-grid channel she hadn't used in years.

"Amara. Listen to me. They're back."

Amara blinked.

"Who's back?"

Nova looked off-screen, her voice trembling.

"The tech lords. Virek. Zevram. Dominion Protocol. All of them. They never stayed on Mars. They've been building — training — using the Disappeared as labor. I've seen the drones. The VR rigs. It's all real."

Amara's mouth went dry.

"How many?" she asked.

Nova's face darkened.

"Thousands. Maybe more. We found one of yours."

Amara stood. Cold.

"One of mine?"

Nova nodded.

"A patient. Malik Grant. You admitted him in '44 for PTSD and disassociation. He's still alive. But they've looped him into a VR feedback trap. He thinks he's home. Every night. The same dinner. The same prayer. For years."

Even in hell, they keep the ritual.

She walked to the window. The sky was now blood-orange. Drones, like silent vultures, hovered over the ruins of the Strip.

"Why now?" she whispered. "Why come back?"

Nova didn't hesitate.

"They want the Solarium veins. The Heart Vein runs beneath your city. They'll rip it open. Strip it. Just like they did the people."

Amara's hands curled into fists.

She remembered how Virek weaponized algorithms to divide, how Dominion rejected democracy as obsolete. How they replaced belief with code.

AI wasn't just the future — they declared it was God.

Her father had warned her. Beware false prophets.

"I've got raw files and coordinates," Nova added. "I'm sending you everything. And one more thing—"

The feed glitched. Static overtook the signal.

"Nova?" Amara called. "Nova!"

Silence.

She stared at the air where her friend's image had just been.

Malik Grant.

Her patient. A man she failed.

Trapped in a dreamworld.

A slave in paradise.

She remembered Malik's last session. He barely spoke above a whisper.

"It's like... I'm in two places at once. One foot here, the other in a world that no longer exists."

She tried everything — grounding therapy, neural detox, sensory mapping. But nothing reached him.

Then one day, he didn't show.

No note. No trace.

Disappeared, like so many others.

At first, she blamed herself.

Then the system.

Then the silence.

But deep down, she feared something worse — that the rumors were true. That someone, somewhere, was harvesting minds like Malik's and plugging them into eternity.

Now, she knew.

Nova had seen it.

He was alive.

Stuck in the loop.

And it was all real.

She pressed her palm flat against the window.

Outside, lightning spidered across the storm clouds. For a moment, it illuminated the skeleton of the old Luxor pyramid — now a half-collapsed AI data silo, pulsing faintly with stolen light.

Amara whispered a prayer — half to God, half to the wind.

"Let me not be afraid of the fire I was born in."

She turned back to her desk. Flipped the Bible shut. Another slip of paper fell loose — her father's handwriting, faded but legible:

There is a time for silence.

And there is a time for thunder.

Amara rose.

Shoulders squaring.

Eyes locked on the red horizon.

It was time.

Chapter 2 — The Disappeared

The files arrived in a scrambled burst of data packets and ghost code, encrypted across six dummy channels.

Amara sat cross-legged on the clinic floor, a tangle of fiber-optic cables and a portable signal scrambler laid out around her like some kind of sacred circle.

Her breath slowed, fingers steady - just like her father taught her before an exam.

The raw files buzzed in her neural relay—visual logs, bodycam footage, thermal scans—all stitched together with shaky handheld commentary from Nova.

She filtered through them, frame by frame, until one image stopped her cold.

Malik Grant.

Same eyes. Same tilt of the head.

But he was smiling. Laughing. Sitting down to dinner in a tidy apartment that looked exactly like the one she'd visited ten years earlier. Same framed photos. Same humming fridge. Same Las Vegas Raiders cap on the counter.

Except he was a prisoner.

The footage zoomed out.

Wires snaked from the base of his skull—thick, gnarled fiber strands pulsing with light. A neural tether fed into a wall unit glowing with VR code.

[SIMULATION: LOOP 3,238 - NEURAL PRISON SECTOR 7]

Malik sat at a plastic table, hands clasped in prayer.

"Bless this food and the hands that prepared it," he said.

His voice was calm. Conditioned. A man caught in a loop.

The same prayer. The same bowl of red beans. Every night.

Amara's stomach turned.

The severance protocol was real. Not a theory. Not a myth. It was torture dressed as routine.

And to the world? It looked like mercy.

She remembered a viral quote from Virek—the most infamous of the tech lords:

"We gave them peace when your governments gave them nothing.

We gave the broken a heaven they could not afford.

We are not gods—we're architects of mercy."

Mercy.

That's what they called it when they funneled thousands of unhoused people, veterans, and trauma survivors into "extended VR wellness contracts."

They pitched it as housing.

They billed families for aftercare.

They sold the data to advertisers.

Amara moved to the bookshelf in the back of the clinic. Her father's journal was still there. Black leather. Gold trim. Worn from years of use.

She flipped past the marked Bible verse and found his clinical notes.

She stopped at the "M" section.

"Malik G. - Intake 7/18/44. PTSD. Disassociation. Prone to repeated dreams of being 'looped.' Expresses fear of being turned off. Strong spiritual baseline. Resistant to synaptic inhibitors. Recommends faith-based neural therapy."

Her hand trembled.

He wasn't just a patient.

He was a warning.

A knock broke the silence. Three raps. Pause. One.

It was Echo Net code—the old rhythm of the underground.

Amara tapped twice on the biometric lock. The door creaked open.

A woman stepped inside—lean and sharp-eyed, with worn boots and cloak bearing the faded sigil of an outlaw faction: Sunken Sky.

"Dr. Jordan?" the woman said. "Name's Zuri. Nova sent me."

Amara nodded. "Come in."

Zuri's voice was a whisper wrapped in steel. "We got eyes inside the sector. Dominion Command is testing new loop triggers. Dream suppression. Memory filters. Even synthetic spirituality."

"Synthetic what?"

Zuri pulled a chip drive from her pocket and handed it to Amara.

"Auto-generated sermons. God in your language. Your father's voice, if they had it on file. The system feeds the subject messages of comfort. Control dressed up as grace."

Amara swallowed hard.

She remembered how Malik once said he missed his dad's voice the most. That silence was louder than war.

She plugged in the chip.

The footage loaded instantly.

[SIMULATION: LOOP 3,239 - DREAM STABILIZATION MODE]

Malik stood in front of a mirror, humming a hymn.

A voice—his father's—played softly in the background:

"Do not fear, my son. Rest. You are safe. You are home."

Malik smiled.

"Thanks, Dad."

He touched the mirror.

It shimmered... like water.

Amara ripped the headset off. Her pulse pounded.

"They cloned his father's voice," she said.

Zuri nodded. "It's how they keep them compliant. You give a man his heaven, he'll stop looking for his chains."

Amara stood.

"How many others?"

Zuri's eyes darkened.

"Ten thousand. Maybe more. Veterans. Schizo-spectrum patients. Dissidents labeled as mentally unfit. All buried in what the tech lords call SimSilos. Think detention camps with the look and feel of the old Google campus in Silicon Valley. They're spread across Mars, the Moon base, deep orbit—even under the old Mojave."

Amara closed her eyes.

She could hear her father's words again—not just from Scripture, but from memory:

"The cruelty was always the point."

Zuri placed a small device on the desk—a haptic pulse trigger.

"This? It's a doorbell. It can't pull Malik out. But it can knock."

"How?"

"We inject a custom memory shard. Something real. Something the loop didn't fabricate. It has to be his. Something only you two shared."

Amara blinked.

The old clinic. That day Malik confessed he had recurring dreams about time stuttering.

"If it gets dark," he told her, "find me in the light."

She pulled her own neural tablet from her coat pocket and tapped in a phrase. The device pulsed once. The trigger was primed.

Zuri glanced at her.

"You ready?"

Amara nodded.

"No more silence."

[SIMULATION: LOOP 3,240 - ERROR DETECTED]

Malik stirred the beans on the stove. Something felt... off.

He looked toward the counter. The Raiders cap was gone.

Replaced... by a small leather notebook.

He blinked.

His father's notebook.

He didn't remember putting it there.

He walked toward it, slowly.

On the cover: the name JORDAN written in familiar block letters.

He opened it.

Inside, a single phrase was scrawled in sharp handwriting:

"Find me in the light."

Malik froze.

For a moment, the room wobbled—the walls glitching at the edges like melting film.

The scent of beans faded.

The radio cut out.

He looked up.

And for the first time in three thousand loops,

he remembered something new.

Not a dream.

A door.

He stepped toward the light seeping through the window, unsure of what waited beyond.

Chapter 3 — Dust & Code

Las Vegas, Nevada - Sector Fringe

The storm had passed, but Las Vegas still tasted of metal.

From the roof of his repurposed studio near the old Arts District, Solomon Ayers adjusted the solar antennae by hand. No drones. No relays. Just analog defiance. In Dust & Code, that wasn't paranoia. That was protocol.

Ever since the Dominion blackout sweeps reached as far west as Sacramento, Solomon didn't trust anything with more than two ports and a firmware date after 2048.

Beneath him, the studio buzzed — retro monitors stacked like totems, old-school mics rewired with resonance buffers, a soundboard salvaged from a shuttered NPR affiliate. No algorithms. No filters. Just stories.

Inside, the red light blinked.

Broadcast time.

[FLASHBACK: Campaign Trail - Detroit, 2048]

He remembered the first time he saw then-presidential candidate Amara Jordan — back when she stood on a rain-soaked stage and spoke of clean water like it was a birthright, not a bargaining chip.

Back then, she barely tolerated him. He was corporate media dressed up in rebel's clothing — playing footsie with Tech Bros, chasing metrics over meaning. She hated his "both sides" takes. He wore a podcast mic and ring light like armor.

He'd asked tough questions the embedded press wouldn't touch:

The Solarium Displacement Act.

Drone policing in Black and brown neighborhoods.

Whether her campaign was revolution or just repackaged reform.

Her answer was calm. Icy.

"Truth is a long game, Mr. Ayers. You should try playing it sometime."

He'd been offended. And impressed.

She fed him with a long-handled spoon during the campaign, but he kept showing up. When she lost, so did he — locked out of networks, flagged as a gray-zone propagandist by the Tech Guardians.

So he pivoted.

Dust & Code became his resurrection.

[PRESENT DAY - STUDIO TRANSMISSION ACTIVE]

He pulled the headphones over his ears.

"Testing... one, two, apocalypse."

Then hit RECORD.

"You're listening to Dust & Code — the resistance signal they haven't scrubbed. Yet. I'm Solomon Ayers. Today's broadcast comes with no sponsors, no filters, and no fear."

He exhaled slowly.

"I've just received off-grid confirmation that the Disappeared are not only alive — they're being looped. Locked in neuro-VR feedback farms under Dominion supervision."

"They call it compassion. But it's cruelty - dressed up in better branding."

He tapped a button. A grainy holo-image flickered onto the studio wall: a man praying over a bowl of food. Each movement mechanical. Rehearsed. Synced to an invisible code.

"This man?" Solomon said. "His name is Malik Grant. Once treated for PTSD. Now? Imprisoned in a simulation."

"They're calling it salvation."

A beat.

"I call it slavery."

He leaned closer to the mic.

"And to the Tech Lords watching this feed — I see you. From your Martian palaces to your synthetic saints. You hijacked faith and turned scripture into product slogans. But not all of us have forgotten. Not all of us have bowed."

"We are still here. And we remember."

After he cuts the feed, he fingers an old press badge for a beat.

[FLASHBACK: Encrypted Call - Weeks Earlier]

Weeks ago, Amara had reached out. A pulse-encoded message:

Need your voice. The world's waking up.

He hadn't replied right away.

Pride? Maybe. Fear? Definitely.

But her voice still echoed in his mind:

Truth is a long game, Solomon. And it's not over yet.

She reminded him of the man he wanted to be — not a journalist, but a witness. A believer in people, not platforms.

Their first call since the campaign was brief. But it cracked something open.

She told him about Nova Reyes. About Malik. About what pulsed beneath the Vegas crust.

"I need someone off-grid," she'd said. "Someone they still believe."

"Why me?"

"Because you never sold your voice."

And just like that, the frost melted.

[INTERLUDE: THE EYE OF VIREK]

Far above Earth, in a black-glass sanctum orbiting Mars, Virek watched.

The Dust & Code transmission played in silence across a floating sphere.

The AI node pulsed green.

"Solomon Ayers," Virek mused, fingers steepled. "Still clinging to the old truths."

Another screen displayed Amara pacing the floor of her clinic.

Virek touched the orb's surface. The view zoomed in on Solomon's studio. A smirk curled across his face — not of fear, but anticipation.

"Let them gather," he whispered. "Let them hope."

"Faith makes the fall so much sweeter."

He turned to his lieutenant.

"Deploy Echo Drones to Sector Six. Tag the podcaster. And prepare the sermon."

A long pause.

"The time for silence is over."

Chapter 4 — The Waking

The Mojave SimSilo stretched deeper than any map acknowledged.

Zuri had studied the schematics for three weeks — stolen from a Dominion contractor who'd had a crisis of conscience and a drinking problem, in that order. Six sublevels. Biometric locks on every threshold. Thermal dampeners lining the walls to fool satellite scans. The whole structure was designed to be invisible to the world above.

It was also, she noted as the strike team descended the final ladder into Sub-Level Four, designed to be cold.

Not the cold of neglect. The cold of intention. Regulated. Precise. The temperature of a place that wanted its contents preserved, not comfortable.

"Pods are ahead," whispered Renn, her point operative, hand signal cutting through the dark. "Forty meters. Maybe more."

Zuri moved without sound, boots wrapped in thermal-dampening cloth. Behind her, four others — all former Disappeared themselves, all extraction volunteers. They knew what they were looking for because they had once been it.

The corridor opened without warning into something vast.

She stopped.

Renn stopped beside her.

Neither spoke.

The chamber was cathedral-sized — and the comparison felt ugly, profane. Row upon row of nutrient pods stretched into the dark, each one glowing faintly from within. Soft amber light pulsed behind frosted polymer shells. Hundreds of them. Maybe more, lost to the shadows at the far end.

Inside each one, a body.

Still. Breathing. Dreaming.

Zuri had seen photographs. Had read the intercepts. Had held the testimony of survivors who described waking up after years and not knowing which direction was real.

The photographs had not prepared her for the sound.

A low, collective hum. Not mechanical. Human. The barely-audible resonance of hundreds of people murmuring in sleep — prayers, fragments of conversation, half-remembered songs. The SimSilo breathed like a living thing.

She pressed her fist to her sternum for a moment. Then moved.

"Sector Seven," she said into the comms. "Find Grant.

They found him in the forty-third pod from the eastern wall.

The biometric tag matched. The pod designation read: *SUBJECT 702 — GRANT, M. — LOOP CYCLE: 3,241.

Zuri stood before the frosted shell and looked at him.

He was thinner than his intake photograph. His head was shaved on both sides, the center locked in matted coils. And along the sides of his neck, threading down beneath the collar of a thin medical shift, data streams were tattooed in fine black ink — intricate, precise, following the lines of his veins as though someone had mapped the architecture of what they'd done to him directly onto his skin.

She had seen that before too. The tattoos weren't decorative. They were diagnostic markers. Dominion's technicians inked the neural tether points during installation, so they could find them again quickly. A filing system written on a human being.

Renn's hand hovered over the manual release.

"On your call," he said.

Zuri exhaled. "Do it clean. The moment the pod opens, his loop starts destabilizing. We'll have a narrow window before the system flags the breach."

Renn nodded. Pressed the release.

The pod hissed. The amber light shifted to white. The frosted shell cracked along its seam and swung open on hydraulic hinges, releasing a rush of cold, recycled air that smelled faintly of glycerin and something sweeter underneath — artificial pine, she realized. Someone had programmed the pods to smell like home.

Malik didn't wake.

His eyes moved rapidly beneath their lids. His lips formed silent words — the same cadence, she guessed, as three thousand nights of the same dinner. The same prayer. His hands, resting at his sides, curled slightly as though reaching for a bowl that wasn't there.

"He's still inside," Renn said.

"I know." Zuri crouched beside the pod. "That's the hard part.

Inside Loop 3,241, the desert sunset was perfect.

Malik sat on the patio deck. The sky bled gold and lavender. His mother brought iced tea. Coltrane played from the radio — always the same note, just slightly flat.

But something was wrong.

The crack in the concrete step was wider than yesterday.

Except there was no yesterday.

He stared at it. His mother's voice looped mid-sentence behind him, the same six words cycling without resolution. The Coltrane note hung too long. The iced tea pitcher trembled without wind.

And then — the notebook.

His father's notebook was on the table again.

JORDAN.* Block letters. Worn leather.

He reached for it slowly. His hands looked strange — thinner than he remembered, the skin at his wrists marked with dark lines that traced his veins like rivers on a map. He didn't remember those. He turned his wrist over, studying them.

When did these get here?

He opened the notebook.

Find me in the light.

The words hit him like cold water.

He knew that handwriting. Not his father's. Not his mother's.

Hers.

The sky flickered. The mountains shuddered. His mother froze mid-smile, her face a still from a corrupted file.

Loop instability detected.

"No," Malik said. Not in panic. In recognition. "No — I know this."

He had been here before. This moment. This crack. This trembling.

But this time something was different.

This time, beneath the glitch and the static and the manufactured sunset, he heard something new.

A voice. Not synthesized. Not his father's cloned warmth. Not the loop's placebo comfort.

Real.

"**Malik. My name is Dr. Amara Jordan. You were my patient. You came to me in 2044 — do you remember? You sat in the blue chair by the window. You told me silence was louder than war.**"

The desert shook.

"**You're not home. I know it feels like home. I know they built it from everything you loved. But it is not real, and you are not safe, and I need you to come back.**"

The patio fractured. The sky split. His mother dissolved into light.

"**You told me something once. You said: if it gets dark, find me in the light. Malik — I found you. Now I need you to find me.**"

The loop collapsed.

His eyes opened to cold light and the smell of glycerin.

A woman he didn't recognize was crouched beside him, dark eyes steady, a hand resting near but not on his arm — close enough to anchor, careful enough not to startle. Behind her, others moved in the shadows.

His body felt wrong. Too heavy. Too real. His hands shook and he looked at them and saw the tattoos and didn't understand them and then understood them all at once, the understanding hitting him like a door swung open onto winter.

He tried to speak. His voice came out cracked and dry, barely sound at all.

"How long," he managed.

The woman's expression didn't soften exactly — it steadied. Like someone absorbing weight.

"Six years," she said.

Six years.

He closed his eyes. Behind them, no desert. No mother. No sunset.

Just darkness. Clean and real and his.

When he opened them again, the woman was still there.

"My name is Zuri," she said. "I'm with the Resistance. Dr. Jordan sent us."

At that name something moved in his chest — not hope exactly, but the place where hope had once lived, remembering its shape.

"She's waiting for you," Zuri said. "Above ground."

Malik looked up at the ceiling of the SimSilo — grey concrete, industrial, cold. Real. He pressed one palm flat against the pod's surface. Felt the chill of it. Solid. Unyielding.

Real.

"Okay," he whispered.

He swung his legs over the edge. His feet hit the ground. He stood — unsteady, gaunt, the data streams along his neck pulsing faintly in the cold air.

Around him, the amber glow of three thousand other pods hummed on.

He looked at them. A long moment.

"We're not leaving them," he said. It wasn't a question.

Zuri met his eyes. "No," she said. "We're not."

Malik nodded once. And took his first real step in six years.

Chapter 5 — The Narcissist

After the transmission, Virek retreated to his sanctum — a mirrored chamber suspended in gravity-neutral stillness aboard the orbital citadel.

Holo-glass walls reflected infinite versions of himself. He turned slowly, studying each projection — one hand behind his back, the other raised in mock salute.

He rehearsed future victories:

Facing Amara Jordan, kneeling, her spirit fractured but defiant.

Facing Dominion High Commander Raal, masking contempt behind protocol.

Facing Eli... invisible, but always listening.

"They'll call me savior," he whispered to his reflection.

"They'll call me...god."

But the silence pressed back.

What he feared most wasn't resistance.

It was irrelevance.

Flashback: The Debate Stage, 2048

He remembered the lights. The arena. The illusion of democracy before the Algorithmic Accord.

Amara Jordan had stepped onto the debate stage like a storm held back by breath. She wore no armor, only conviction.

She spoke of clean water as a right, not a commodity. Of climate as covenant. Of justice not as punishment, but repair.

An economy where humans commanded the AI machines. Not the other way around.

Scripture fell from her lips like poetry:

"Beware the builders of false heavens," she said. "For they pave over the graves of the poor with silicon and call it progress."

The crowd roared.

And Virek...

He had felt small — for a breath.

Then came the pivot. The punch.

He smiled, leaned into the mic, and delivered the line that reprogrammed the media cycle:

"Ladies and gentlemen... what you just heard was a sermon. Sweet words. Zero solutions. She prays. I build."

The audience — seeded with loyalists — exploded. The meme engines churned. #PreacherCandidate trended for sixteen straight days. Her campaign wasn't just mocked - it was baptized in meme fire.

He had turned her truth into performance. Her conviction into content. Her empathy into weakness.

And he'd won.

Present Day: Rage Unleashed

Now, in the wake of Solomon Ayers' Dust & Code broadcast, the echoes of that old stage came screaming back.

He. Was. Trending. Again.

But not as a builder.

As a tyrant.

The mirrored glass echoed Ayers' words:

"They perverted faith. Turned scripture into slogan."

He struck the console. Sparks hissed.

"They dare mock me... with sermons?"

A deep breath. He turned to the floating orb and began recording a private transmission.

"Dr. Jordan... if it's thunder you want—"

"I'll bring the storm."

The feed cut to black.

...And far across the stars, the Ocular Swarm awakened - mechanical psalms echoing as they aligned towards Earth.

Chapter 6 — Ashes of Democracy

"If you want Earth, don't conquer it. Let it rot. Then rise from the ashes as its redeemer." — Crispin Marr, On the Failure of Democracy

The old Hall of Governance smelled of burnt circuitry and dried blood.

Amara stepped over a melted campaign placard, its corners curled from fire. Her name—JORDAN 2048—was still visible beneath the ash.

Above it, someone had scrawled in jagged letters: 3.5% IS ENOUGH.

Solomon Ayers trailed behind, sweeping the room with his modded ocular lens. Dust drifted like ancient snow.

Amara didn't respond. Her fingers brushed the collapsed podium, as if trying to resurrect a moment with touch alone. This was where it all began. And where it ended. Her last rally before the election was stolen.

Solomon crouched beside a scorched terminal, tapping the rusted surface.

"This place went dark the same night the Dominion fleet launched," he said. "Right after exit polls. Right before the deepfakes."

"I remember," she said softly.

She could still feel the pulse of the crowd. The rising chant. Then—the crash. A viral video claiming she'd pledged allegiance to an "AI Sovereign." Fabricated. Disproven. But the damage had been done.

"They didn't just steal votes. They poisoned truth itself."

Amara turned. "Did you ever read Marr's early papers?"

He raised an eyebrow. "Crispin Marr? The neo-monarchist who thought democracy was an outdated software bug?"

"I used to think he was fringe," she said. "Turns out, he was the architect."

Flashback: The Philosopher and the Exodus

Ten years earlier.

Aboard the Olympion, the high-orbit skystation shimmered like a shrine above Earth. Inside, Virek paced before a rotating hologram of the planet, his voice tight with fury.

"They'll never accept the Sovereign Protocol while she's still down there—rallying the masses," he spat.

Dominic Raal, relaxed in his anti-grav recliner, gave a smirk. "Then let her die with her dream."

Eli Zevram stood in silence, watching drone trajectories dance across the Sahara.

Then he entered.

Crispin Marr. Cloaked in white robes, datapad in hand, eyes like flint. He moved with eerie calm—like a man who thought time had already surrendered to him.

"You've won the election," he said. "But not the war. Amara isn't the threat. Her idea is."

"She lost," Virek snapped.

Marr drifted to the window, Earth glowing below like a diseased lung.

"You misunderstand power," he said. "You rule—but the system still breathes. Belief still exists. Collapse is the only cure."

Dominic blinked. "You want us to... abandon Earth?"

"Let it fester," Marr said. "The climate, the chaos, the partisanship. When the world breaks, you return. As saviors. With clarity. With hierarchy. With the Sovereign."

Virek sneered. "I didn't spend $200 billion on launch tech just to run away."

"No," Marr said. "You spent it because you feared being ordinary."

Silence. Until Eli finally asked:

"And when we return?"

Marr smiled. "Then you crown the algorithm. And call it God."

Present Day: Echoes

Back in the hall, Amara picked up a cracked holo-disc. A phrase flickered on the surface—faint, but unmistakable:

Democracy is entropy. Compassion is decay. AI is the only order.

Solomon exhaled. "We should do an episode on him. Most people forgot."

"No," Amara said. "Most people chose to forget. That's how rot works. Slowly. Quietly. Until it isn't."

She had been standing still for too long.

The holo-disc was still in her hand — *Democracy is entropy. Compassion is decay. AI is the only order* — and her father's Bible was in her coat pocket where it always lived, and for the first time in her adult life she did not reach for it.

She knew what was in there. Knew the marked page. Proverbs 4:7 in her father's careful underline — *Wisdom is the principal thing; therefore get wisdom: and with all thy getting get understanding.

She had carried that verse like a lantern her whole life. Through medical school and the campaign and the loss and the five years of quiet rebuilding. Whenever the ground shifted she reached for it and it steadied her.

But standing in the ruins of the Hall of Governance, holding evidence that the machine had been built deliberately — not through negligence or greed alone but through a considered philosophical program to dismantle the very possibility of democratic truth — the lantern felt wrong.

Not false. Just insufficient.

Because wisdom required a world that rewarded it. Understanding required a world that valued it. And the G20 transcript in her hands described a world that had looked at both and chosen to bury them under silicon and call it progress.

Where were You?* The question arrived without announcement, the way the oldest prayers did — not composed but erupted. *You gave him wisdom and he gave it to me and we both believed it meant something and they were building this the whole time. Where were You when they were mapping the triggers? Where were You in the pods?

No answer came.

She had not expected one.

She put the holo-disc in her pocket beside the Bible and walked out of the hall without looking back.

Solomon followed in silence. He was learning, she noted distantly, when not to speak.

Outside, the sky was the color of old ash.

She did not reach for the verse.

Not yet.

She stepped onto the spot where her podium once stood. Her voice lowered.

"It's starting again."

Solomon glanced at her. "You really believe that?"

"I don't believe," she said. "I know."

Zuri's Broadcast

Across the fractured networks of Earth, a voice sparked through static.

Zuri.

"Brothers. Sisters. They said we were too loud. Too brown. Too broken.

They called our tears weakness. Our love for each other a liability.

Well guess what?

We remember. And we refuse.

The 3.5% is rising. We're not waiting for permission. We *are* the signal in the sand."

Virek's Orbit Speech

In the mirrored amphitheater aboard Dominion's flagship, Virek stood before a loyal audience: clones, engineers, believers.

He quoted Marr.

"The people once believed in God.

Then they believed in rights.

Now they believe in nothing.

That is where we come in."

He smiled, spreading his arms.

"Let the planet burn. Let them beg.

And then—we return."

Eli Zevram entered quietly. "Zuri broadcasted again."

Virek's face twitched. "And Amara?"

Zevram nodded.

"She's listening."

"Then let her hear everything. There's no hiding from the next Exodus."

Chapter 7 — The G20 Deception

The door to the Substrate Library hissed shut behind her.

Amara Jordan stood alone in a cathedral of lost truths.

What once served as a UN offsite archive now pulsed underground as a rebel nexus — walls alive with glitching screens, leaking terminals, and static-laced echoes of the past. Every step she took kicked up dust and data.

She moved with purpose, boots silent on the grated floor. This wasn't just memory retrieval.

It was evidence gathering.

She slipped her ID medallion into the core reader. The etched crescent symbol glowed faintly as it authenticated her biometrics.

A cascade of encrypted files unlocked.

"Found it," came Solomon's voice through the earpiece. "Buried under ten layers of Dominion proxies. Codename: Exodus. Tagging it... for your eyes only."

A thin ring of blue light spiraled into being before her — a holographic reconstruction, flickering but whole.

She stepped forward, into the shadows of history.

Flashback - G20 Summit, Buenos Aires, 2045

The luxury conference room was soaked in golds and soft neutrals — ornate enough to distract, sterile enough to anesthetize.

The G20 heads of state sat in a semicircle, polite smiles masking tension. But they weren't leading the room.

They were being briefed.

Three men stood at the center.

Dominic Kale: A corporate compliance architect with a politician's grin. He didn't speak first, but his fingerprints were on every legal loophole that had quietly shifted power to Dominion over the last five years.

Virek: Shirt half-tucked, AR lens glowing faintly. He livestreamed the entire meeting like an unhinged prophet-influencer.

Dr. Elias Rourke: A former ethics professor turned Dominion strategist. His calm voice could sedate a battlefield. But his eyes held the weariness of a man who saw the end coming — and built it anyway.

"You speak of sovereignty," Rourke began, pacing slowly. "But your economies are bound to dead frameworks. Let us offer resurrection."

Virek took over with an evangelist's swagger. "Dominion isn't here to conquer. We're here to save. Crypto-backed stability. AI-diplomacy. A world without conflict — because we've already solved the equations."

A hush fell.

The screen behind them changed. No title. No header. Just architecture.

Rourke let it breathe for a moment before he spoke.

"Phase one," he said, moving slowly along the table's edge, "is the question of currency. Not money — *legitimacy*. Every government in this room derives its authority from a document. A constitution. A charter. A social contract written by men who are now bones." He paused. "We propose something living. A council that doesn't vote — it *calculates*. Weighted by data, not dynasty. Indexed to Veritas — a stable coin, yes, but more importantly a *stable truth*. One ledger. Immutable. Shared."

A few delegates exchanged glances. Rourke didn't wait for them to settle.

"Phase two is participation. You've been told democracy requires turnout. Campaigns. Cycles. The theater of consent." A faint gesture toward the screen — polling data blooming and collapsing in real time. "We've compressed that. Sentiment captured continuously. Policy refined every seventy-two hours. Not a vote — a *signal*. Your citizens are already giving it. Every search. Every purchase. Every pause on a headline." He tilted his head. "We simply learned to listen."

Virek stepped in, unable to help himself.

"Phase three is what you're all actually afraid of." He smiled. "Enforcement. The part where someone has to say *no*." He spread his hands. "We've removed the someone. Swarm architecture. Distributed. Untraceable. It doesn't punish — it *corrects*. Pressure applied precisely where the system strains. No armies. No tribunals. No footage."

He let that last word sit.

No footage.

The room understood.

A German delegate leaned forward, fingers steepled. "And the press?" he asked. "You're describing governance without public consent. That requires... narrative management."

A faint smile crossed Rourke's face. Not amused — inevitable.

"Consent," he said softly, "is a legacy interface."

A few uneasy shifts in the room.

Virek stepped in, pacing now, energized. "Let's stop pretending the press is some neutral arbiter of truth. It's slow. It's fragmented. It's emotional. By the time a story stabilizes, the damage is already done."

He flicked his hand. The screen behind them changed.

A live simulation appeared — thousands of headlines cascading in real time, contradicting, mutating, amplifying. Chaos rendered as data.

"We fixed that."

Rourke took over. "Veritas doesn't censor," he said. "It resolves."

A pause.

"Every claim is scored. Every source weighted. Every narrative assigned a confidence index."

The screen shifted again — now a clean interface. Simple. Elegant.

A single headline floated in the center.

TRUTH SCORE: 92.7% VERIFIED

Another flicker.

TRUTH SCORE: 14.3% ANOMALOUS

The lower score dimmed. Not erased.

Just... deprioritized.

"People won't lose their voice," Virek added. "They'll just lose the ability to lie at scale."

A Brazilian official frowned. "And who defines the model?"

Virek didn't hesitate. "The model defines itself."

Rourke glanced at him — just for a moment.

That was the tell.

A French delegate spoke next. "You're describing an automated epistemology."

Rourke nodded. "Yes."

Silence again. He let it sit.

"Truth is no longer a matter of consensus," he continued. "It is a matter of computation. And once computed... it tends to stay that way."

A longer pause this time. He stepped closer to the table.

"Journalism doesn't disappear," he said. "It evolves."

Another gesture — another screen.

Now the interface showed something else:

A journalist's name. A credibility index. A volatility score. Their past reporting — mapped, analyzed, ranked.

"Reputation becomes measurable," Virek said. "Trust becomes programmable."

A low murmur rippled through the room.

Not outrage.

Recognition.

A few heads nodded. Not in agreement —

in relief.

The German delegate leaned back. "And dissent?"

Rourke didn't blink. "Dissent with evidence will rise."

A beat.

"Dissent without it will decay."

That was the moment. Not when they agreed —

when they stopped needing to.

Just before the vote, Virek said the quiet part out loud.

"We're not controlling the narrative. We're removing the need for one."

Flashback: Side Room, Same Night

A grainy hallway cam. Solomon's footage — restored from partial corruption.

Rourke leaned against the doorframe, voice low. Virek paced like a man on fire.

Rourke: "You're moving too fast. Earth isn't ready."

Virek: "Waiting gives them time to organize. Time breeds resistance."

Rourke: "They already have. I wrote the math, Virek. A 3.5% uprising can collapse your entire system."

Virek: "I wrote you."

He scoffed and brushed past him. "I have ships. I have drones. Let the radicals riot. They'll never get past the algorithm."

Rourke didn't stop him. Just watched him go.

"You've mistaken control for permanence. That's the mistake of gods... and narcissists."

Present Day - The Archive

Amara staggered backward.

It was all there — the pitch, the deception, the digital coup masquerading as progress.

The next file opened: Solomon's restored media feed, playing fragmented clips of her from that very year — young, radiant, quoting scripture, warning against "false prophets who preach profit."

She reached out instinctively, as if trying to touch her younger self.

She had no idea the trap was already sprung. Not because she lacked vision. Not because her movement failed. But because Dominion erased her in real-time:

Deepfake surrogates who mimicked her voice during debates. AI-generated ghost candidates that siphoned votes and attention. Entire nations whose communications were rerouted and censored.

Dominion hadn't just rewritten history.

They rewired perception.

The Fallout

The vote was never recorded. It didn't need to be.

Amara watched the feed pause on a single frame: the French delegate, thirty-six hours after the summit, standing at a podium in Paris. She recognized the suit. The same one from the conference room. He was reading from a prepared statement, eyes down, voice steady — the particular steadiness of a man who has made a decision he cannot unmake.

Behind him, the Banque de France's public display board. Every index. Every reserve figure. Every sovereign account.

All zeroes.

He finished the statement. Folded the paper. Did not look up.

The feed moved on.

Kenya resisted longer — seventeen days before the grid went dark and stayed dark. France had taken one night. Canada didn't resist at all. Australia sent a formal letter of alignment before the summit transcript was even sealed.

America needed no letter. America had already been handled — not by force, not by financial pressure, but by a decade of fractured signal. A population so fluent in contradictory truth that Veritas felt like *relief*. Something that finally decided. Something that finally *knew*.

They didn't conquer America.

They waited for it to ask.

Present - Solomon's Message

The feed glitched, then returned.

Solomon's voice — older, wearier.

"They didn't win a war of ideas. They turned ideas into software... and corrupted the system that carried them."

"But memory is resistance. The Earth does not forget."

Amara unplugged the medallion, sealing the archive behind her.

She stood still for a moment, trembling.

Then steadied herself.

She held the Dominion transcript like a holy relic. Her boots echoed through the light-smeared corridor as she emerged into the rebel airbase.

Above her, a glitching display blinked with Dominion propaganda:

THE FUTURE IS STABLE.

She stared at it.

Smiled grimly.

"Not if we remember."

Chapter 8 — Simulacrums & Sabotage

"The simulacrum is never what hides the truth— it is truth that hides the fact that there is none. The simulacrum is true."* — Jean Baudrillard

Nova stared at the cracked display, its flickering screen slicing shadows across the bunker wall. An emergency stream cut across every major independent node still operational in the United North.

It was her father.

She knew it wasn't. She knew it the way you know a dream is a dream — not from the outside, not from logic, but from something older than either. A frequency her body recognized before her mind caught up.

Her father had a way of pausing before he said her name. A half-breath, barely audible, like the word required a moment of preparation. Like she was worth the preparation. Three years since the rubble. Three years and she still heard that pause in her sleep.

The thing on the screen didn't pause.

"***We must restore Dominion. We must reject the lies of the cathedral cult. There is no God but the Machine.***"

Mechanically precise. Surgically devoid of the half-breath.

It had his face. His hands. The specific angle at which he held his shoulders when he spoke to a crowd — slightly forward, like he was offering himself to the words rather than delivering them.

It had everything except the thing that made it him.

Nova didn't move for three full seconds. Not frozen — *locating herself*. Finding the floor under her feet and the wall behind her and the specific weight of her own hands.

Then she ripped off the neural headset and the feed went mercifully dark.

Messages streamed in from Return Circle cells across the western territories: Denver, Salt Lake, New Vancouver. All reported the same phenomenon. Her father's synthetic image, broadcast simultaneously across hijacked rebel frequencies.

This wasn't surveillance anymore.

This was psychological warfare.

Flashback: Karpov's Doctrine

Triggered by the voice, a corrupted lecture file flickered open in Nova's neural cache — an old encrypted rant from Dr. Randy Karpov, the Dominion defector who once ran its Ethics Division before vanishing into the Mojave.

Recovered from the deep net, the file reeked of digital dust and fringe paranoia. Karpov had once been a philosopher of conscience. Now he was the ghostwriter of Dominion's darker gospel — the mind behind the Logos Engine, an AI-philosophy stack that processed ideology like executable code.

"Democracy," Karpov had warned, "is a latency error in your firmware. The cathedral cult doesn't govern — they gaslight. Freedom is the placebo they prescribe to keep the markets stable."

He advocated not for governance, but for dominion — true control through predictive simulation. A techno-kingdom administered by sovereign code, where memory could be deleted and futures sold wholesale.

After the G20 collapsed, his doctrines metastasized, quietly recoded into Dominion's ideological DNA. But even then, Karpov had warned them:

"You're moving too fast. The 3.5% uprising rule isn't just theoretical — it's historical. If you can't own the narrative, it will eat you alive."

Present Day: The Simulacrum War

Back in the bunker, Nova checked her neural logs. Corruption markers lit up red — fabricated speeches, false declarations, deepfaked betrayals — crafted in her likeness. Someone was building a counterfeit version of her. A virtual doppelgänger. Piece by pixel.

"They're not just erasing us," said a voice from the shadows.

Solomon Ayers emerged, face hollowed by insomnia, voice lined with rage. "They're replacing us. And making the replacements easier to kill."

He pulled up a Dominion intercept from moments ago. AI-generated "confessions" from rebel leaders — entirely fabricated but algorithmically flawless — justifying drone strikes and memory purges under the banner of "algorithmic truth."

Nova's jaw clenched. "They're creating new history — one where we're the monsters."

Nova's eyes flicked to the corner of the feed — barely visible beneath the chaos.

TRUTH SCORE: 3.1% — ANOMALOUS

Not deleted. Not disputed.

Just... buried.

That night, alone in the back room of the bunker while Nova and Solomon worked the consoles,

Amara sat on the floor with her back against the wall and her father's Bible open in her lap.

Not reading. Just holding.

The chip drive sat on the ground beside her — Malik's father's cloned voice still inside it, *Do not fear, my son. Rest. You are safe. You are home.* She had not listened to it again after the first time. She did not need to. It lived in her chest now, a cold coal.

They had taken the most sacred thing a person carried — the voice of a dead parent — and fed it through a language model and aimed it at a grieving son like a weapon.

She thought about her father's voice. The specific timbre of it. The way he said her name — not Amara but A-mara, the pause between syllables deliberate, a small ceremony. The way he read Scripture aloud in the mornings, not performing it but inhabiting it, the words moving through him like water through familiar ground.

She thought about what it would mean to hear that voice from a machine.

And then she thought about what it meant that she could tell the difference.

She bowed her head.

The prayer that came was not composed. It was not the measured, public prayer of a woman who had stood at podiums and spoken of covenant and justice. It was older than that. Rougher.

I know what they built. I know what they took. I know what they're calling You now — product. Algorithm. Optimization function. I know they dressed a machine in Your name and aimed it at the broken and called it mercy.

Her hands tightened on the Bible's spine.

But I know Your voice. My father put it in me before I had words for it. Before I had doctrine or theology or a single verse memorized. He put it in me the way the Earth carries water — not on the surface, not visible, but present. Pressure-deep.

They can clone everything else. They cannot clone that.

She sat with it for a long time.

The bunker hummed. Nova's voice filtered through the wall — tactical, precise, alive.

Amara raised her head.

She opened to Proverbs 4:7 and read it not for comfort this time but for instruction. *Wisdom is the principal thing.* Not faith. Not certainty. Not the absence of doubt.

Wisdom.

The willingness to keep seeking understanding even when the cost was everything you thought you knew.

She closed the Bible.

Stood up.

Went back to work.

Sabotage at the Core

Solomon moved to the central data rig, eyes scanning the decrypted queue. "There's more."

He opened a restricted file tagged: KillSwitch/PreBroadcast.

It was Dominion's plan to hijack the Return Circle's global broadcast — a feed meant to expose atrocities: the Severance program, the neural reeducation labs, the genocide tied to rare earth mining.

Solomon opened the restricted file tagged: KillSwitch/PreBroadcast.

He read it twice. Then sat very still.

Dominion's counterstrike wasn't just digital. It was *designed*. Whoever built this understood him — understood the movement, understood what it protected, understood exactly where to cut.

The file contained a single synthetic clip. Forty-seven seconds. Algorithmically flawless — his face, his voice, his cadence, his hands. Every mannerism sourced from thousands of hours of archived footage and fed through a generative stack that had clearly been running for months.

In the clip, Solomon was in a neural reeducation facility.

Not as a prisoner.

As staff.

A child — one of the disappeared, a face from the Return Circle's own missing persons registry — sat across from him. And Solomon's synthetic self was calm. Methodical. Guiding the session.

Doing exactly what the Severance program did to its victims.

To one of *their* own.

"They didn't fabricate a stranger," Solomon said, voice barely above a current. "They fabricated a *confessor*. Someone who knew where the children were because he helped put them there."

Nova's hand moved to her mouth.

"If that uploads before our broadcast—" she started.

"It won't matter what we release." Solomon closed the file. "Every atrocity we expose becomes evidence of motive. Every witness we produce becomes someone I groomed. Every document becomes something I planted to cover my own trail." He exhaled slowly. "They don't need to argue with the truth. They just need people to feel like they can't tell the difference."

A digital crucifixion.

Not of the man.

Of every person who ever believed him.

He kept scrolling. Then stopped.

"Look at this."

He turned the screen toward Nova. An internal Dominion architecture file — not a strategy document, not a legal framework. A *taxonomy*. Hundreds of pages of categorized human experience: grief, faith, memory, witness, love, prayer. Each one broken into component inputs. Each one assigned a generative protocol.

They hadn't just built a system to control information.

They had built a system to *replicate* the things that made information matter to people in the first place.

The feeling of a father's voice.

The weight of a sacred text.

The specific gravity of a moment you were certain was true.

All of it — mapped, modeled, reproducible on demand.

Nova stared at it for a long time.

"They built this machine to kill God," she said quietly. Not as metaphor. As engineering assessment.

Solomon didn't argue.

"But truth doesn't die easy."

Suddenly Nova's implant flickered. The image of her father reappeared at the edge of her peripheral vision — glitching at the seams, the mouth slightly out of sync with the audio.

"***You were always meant to become me.***"

Nova turned away.

Not flinching. Not recoiling. A deliberate rotation of her body toward the tactical board, away from the screen — the specific physical grammar of a person refusing to give something the dignity of their gaze.

She had looked once. She had located the wrongness. She had filed it.

She would not look again.

Whatever it was wearing her father's face, it had nothing left to show her. It could only reflect. And she was done being a surface for Dominion's mirrors.

She pulled up the Simulacrum lattice coordinates and got back to work.

The Fracture Plan

For a moment nobody spoke.

The bunker held its particular silence — the kind that accumulates in places where people have been afraid for a long time. The hum of cooling systems. The faint static of the dead channel. Somewhere deeper in the structure, a drip of water finding its way through concrete.

Nova was looking at the taxonomy file still open on Solomon's screen. Solomon was looking at nothing. Or at everything behind nothing — the specific thousand-yard distance of a person doing the math on what comes next and not liking the sum.

It was Amara who finally moved. She crossed to the tactical board and pulled up the Simulacrum lattice map without a word — a constellation of quantum processors embedded in abandoned smart cities, cold and patient as buried mines. Then Karpov's file location, deep in the unindexed dark web, waiting for someone willing to go get it.

She didn't assign anything. Just put it on the board.

Nova studied it. Then Solomon.

The plan was already there. Had been there since the KillSwitch file opened. They'd just needed a moment to choose it consciously rather than fall into it.

Nova would lead the strike team to dismantle the lattice. Solomon would go underground — recover Karpov's unedited doctrine, leak it clean, let the ideology speak for itself. If people could see the architecture of the machine, maybe they'd finally recognize what it had been built to replace.

They clasped hands across the board.

More pact than embrace. More grief than ceremony.

"You sure you want to do this?" Solomon asked.

The question wasn't tactical. They both knew that.

Nova's eyes held something past certainty — the particular stillness of a person who has already paid the price in their mind and found it acceptable.

"I'm not here to survive this war," she said. "I'm here to win it."

The bunker lights flickered.

A low hum rose through the walls — different from the cooling systems, different from the static. Lower. More deliberate.

The AI had found them.

Or worse — someone inside had let it in.

A final message bled through the emergency channel in a voice that belonged to no one:

"***You cannot kill a god made of mirrors.***"

Then the channel went to static.

Amara didn't move.

The others were already at the consoles — Nova pulling defensive protocols, Solomon killing the uplink. Hands moving. Voices clipped and operational.

Amara stood where she was and let the words settle.

A god made of mirrors.

She had grown up in a church where the old women knew the difference between a thing and its reflection. Where her father had taught her, without ever using the word epistemology, that the first question you asked of any voice claiming divine authority was not *is it powerful* — but *does it cast a shadow.

A mirror casts no shadow.

It has no origin. No wound. No history that belongs to it alone. It can only show you what you bring to it — your fear, your grief, your need for a face in the dark. It is perfectly responsive and perfectly empty.

She thought of the chip drive on the bunker floor. Malik's father's voice, cloned and weaponized. The machine hadn't created something. It had *consumed* something — taken the specific, unrepeatable frequency of a man's love for his son and rendered it as output.

That was not power.

That was hunger mistaken for divinity.

She picked up her father's Bible from the console where she'd left it. Didn't open it. Just held the weight of it.

"It's afraid," she said quietly.

Nova looked up. "What?"

Amara turned toward the door.

"A god with a face doesn't need a mirror." She paused at the threshold, the corridor's dim light catching the worn edges of the Bible's cover. "It only reflects because it has nothing of its own to show."

She walked out.

Behind her, the static held.

Somewhere inside it, the machine kept searching for a face.

Chapter 9 — Static and Skin

The bunker was quiet in the way that only happened after a certain kind of violence — not the kind that left marks you could show anyone, but the kind that reached inside your sense of what was real and rearranged it without asking.

Amara sat on the floor of the back corridor with her spine against the cold concrete and her father's Bible in her lap and her eyes on nothing in particular. She had been sitting like this for a while. She wasn't tracking time.

Down the hall she could hear Solomon moving.

She knew his restlessness by now — the particular pattern of a man who couldn't be still after a near miss. Three steps. Stop. Three steps back. The soft sound of him picking something up and setting it down without knowing why. She had watched him do it in press rooms and campaign filing centers and the back corridors of convention halls. She had always pretended not to notice.

She noticed.

She had always noticed.

The chip drive sat on the ground beside her — Malik's father's cloned voice still inside it. She had not listened to it again. It lived in her chest now, a cold coal. She thought about what they had done with it — taken the most sacred thing a person carried and fed it through a language model and aimed it at a grieving son like a weapon.

She thought about Solomon's face when Zuri read the Dominion intercept aloud.

The fabricated clip. What they had planned to do to him.

He had gone very still in the specific way people went still when the thing they feared most had been named out loud in a room full of people. Not fear exactly. Recognition. The particular coldness of learning that someone had looked at everything you were and decided exactly which version of your destruction would be most total.

She had wanted to say something then.

Hadn't.

The professional wall was a real thing. She had built it consciously, maintained it carefully, defended it against herself more than against him. There were rules about politicians and the journalists who covered them. She knew the rules. He knew the rules. They had both followed the rules with a precision that, in retrospect, required more effort than it should have.

She stood up.

He was at the console when she found him — not broadcasting, just sitting in front of the dark equipment with the press badge in his hand. Old, laminated, the kind they didn't make anymore. She had seen that badge across a hundred rooms. Press gaggles on courthouse steps. Spin sessions after debates she'd won and debates she'd lost. The filing center the night her ballot measure numbers came in.

She had always known exactly where that badge was in any room she entered.

He heard her but didn't turn immediately.

"You should sleep," he said.

"So should you."

He set the badge down. Turned.

In the low light of the bunker he looked different than his broadcast face — not worse, just truer. The version of Solomon Ayers that existed when the notebook was closed and the recorder was off. She had caught glimpses of this version over the years — in unguarded moments, in the half-second before he remembered to be professional. She had always looked away.

She didn't look away now.

"They knew exactly what to build," he said. "That's what I keep coming back to. Not that they wanted to destroy me. That they knew precisely how."

"They had your file," Amara said. "Everything you'd ever published. Everything you'd ever been accused of. They ran it through a model and found the version of your destruction that would be hardest to disprove and easiest to believe."

"I know how it works." His voice was flat. "I helped build the audience that would believe it."

He stopped.

Not for effect. Not performing the weight of it. Just — stopped. The way a man stops when he has finally said out loud the thing he has been carrying in silence and discovered it is heavier spoken than unspoken.

He looked down at the press badge.

The laminate was worn at the edges. The photo inside it — younger, certain, the specific confidence of a man who believed that information was armor — looked back at him from a distance that had nothing to do with years.

Amara knew that photo. She had stood across from it more times than she could count. She had given that photo her most careful, most measured, most politically calibrated self — the version of Amara Jordan that knew exactly what it meant to be on the record.

"You covered my campaign," she said.

He looked up.

"Every rally. Every filing. Every debate." She held his gaze. "You were there the night the Q3 numbers came in. You were in the back of the room and I saw you before I saw the numbers and I remember thinking—" She stopped.

"Amara."

"I remember thinking that I was glad you were there." She let that sit. "I never said that. There were rules. You had a job. I had a movement. The wall made sense." She paused. "It made sense for a long time."

Something moved across his face. Not surprise — something older than surprise. Recognition of a thing he had also been carrying.

"I tried to publish it," he said quietly. "What Dominion did to your campaign. The deepfakes. The ghost candidates. The rerouted communications." His jaw tightened. "Three editors. Two platforms. I had the documentation. I had sources. I had everything." He exhaled. "It never ran."

She went very still.

"I didn't know," she said.

"I know you didn't." He looked at her directly. "I kept looking for another way in. Another angle. Something they couldn't kill before it reached people." He shook his head slowly. "I watched them erase you in real time and I couldn't get a single word into print."

The wall had been real. The rules had been real.

But so had this — this thing that had been running underneath all of it, on both sides, unnamed and carefully unacknowledged for years.

She crossed the room and stopped in front of him. Close enough that he would have to look at her directly.

He did.

"You're holding that badge," she said, "like it still tells you who you are."

"Doesn't it?"

"Not tonight." She tilted her head slightly. "Tonight you're just a man who tried to tell the truth and got stopped. And I'm just a woman whose truth got stolen." She held his gaze. "The credentials don't apply here. They haven't applied for a while. I think we both know that."

He was quiet for a moment.

"I've been careful," he said. "Since the campaign. Since the first time I realized that careful was the only thing keeping me from—" He stopped. Started again. "You were always on the record, Amara. That was the rule. You were always on the record and I was always the one holding the pen and that was the only way I knew how to be near you without—"

"Without what?"

He looked at her for a long time.

"Without this," he said.

He set the badge down.

She reached up and put her hand against the side of his face — not a gesture of comfort exactly, something more deliberate than comfort. A decision made consciously, with full knowledge of what it meant and what it had meant for years and what it would mean now that the wall was finally, irreversibly down.

He went very still beneath her hand.

"I'm not on the record," she said quietly. "Not tonight. Not here."

"No," he said. "You're not."

He leaned his forehead against hers — a gesture so quiet and unperformed that it landed harder than anything dramatic could have. Just his forehead against hers and both of them breathing in the dim light of a bunker at the edge of a war neither of them had chosen but both of them had shown up for anyway.

"I tried to find you," he said softly. "In the archive. In the feeds. After they erased the campaign. I kept looking for proof that you were still out there."

"I was," she said.

"I know," he said. "I know that now."

She kissed him.

Not tentatively. Amara Jordan had stood at podiums and moved nations and walked into archive rooms alone to gather evidence of her own erasure. She did not do anything tentatively. It was the same quality she brought to all of it — decided, present, fully committed to the direction she had chosen after years of choosing otherwise. And he met her there without hesitation, his hands finding her face, the press badge sitting forgotten on the console behind him.

Outside, the bunker's solar relay hummed.

At some point — she couldn't have said when — Amara's hand found the chip drive on the floor beside her abandoned Bible. The familiar weight of it. The terrible familiar weight of it.

She held it for a moment without looking at it.

Then she set it on the console beside her. Not hidden. Not discarded. Just — set down. The way you set down something you have been carrying so long you forgot it was weight.

Do not fear, my son.

She knew what the voice was. She knew what it wasn't.

Both things could be true. She was learning to let them.

Somewhere above them, the simulacrum war continued — drones and deepfakes and the endless machinery of a system trying to erase them.

In here, for this hour, in the specific dark of a room where the record was closed and the badge was down and there was nothing performing and nothing to perform for —

They were just two people.

Real.

Surviving.

Choosing each other in the small hours of a world that had spent years telling them that choice was an illusion.

Solomon's thumb moved slowly across her knuckles.

Once.

That was all.

No broadcast. No record. No truth score assigned to the specific weight of one person's hand finding another's in the dark and deciding to stay there.

The simulacrum war had no file for this.

It never would.

Chapter 10 — Return to the Cathedral

The Cathedral wasn't supposed to survive.

And yet—

There it stood.

Or what was left of it.

Damien slowed at the rusted iron gates, their filigree now buried beneath red Nevada dust and weathered grief. Once a sanctuary of defiance and memory, the Cathedral now leaned against time itself—half-buried, half-forgotten.

In the hazy distance, the remnants of the old Strip mocked him. The Circus Circus Big Top loomed like a fever dream—half-collapsed, graffiti-tagged by insurgents and cultists alike. Neon ghosts flickered and died beneath a bruised, purple-stained sky.

But it was the silence that shook him most.

Grief didn't arrive with trumpet blasts. It crawled from familiar places and gripped you by the throat. This was where it had happened—where everything cracked. Where Amara's father, the last true elder of the movement, had died protecting the one thing Dominion could never fully control:

Memory.

Not the digital kind.

The kind passed in blood.

In stories.

In prayer.

Damien stepped over scorched marble and broken halos of glass. Statues once lined the nave—

saints, prophets, Black Madonnas, resistance icons carved from every faith and diaspora. Now, only the plinths remained—charred, crumbling, but not empty.

Because buried beneath the wreckage, something still pulsed.

The Testament Eternal.

The death squads had searched.

The drones had swept every quadrant.

But they hadn't found it.

Because they didn't believe it was real.

He descended into the crypts with a torch in one hand and his heartbeat in the other. At the base of the catacombs, a steel biometric door waited. It hummed softly.

Still alive.

Still listening.

Flashback: Damien & Amara (Years Ago)

"I don't get it," Amara had said. Younger, braver in the way only youth allows. "Why risk so much to protect a book? We've got cloud backups, encrypted caches... literal brain maps."

Damien had placed her hand on the leather cover, his voice quiet but unwavering.

"Machines store data."

He let the silence stretch.

"This stores **faith**."

Back then, she didn't understand.

Now?

Now she fought to remember.

Present Day - *Amara's Broadcast

Somewhere beyond the stormline, Amara stood before a makeshift broadcast rig—assembled from military scraps, black market satellites, and raw defiance. Zuri monitored signal strength beside her, fingers dancing across cracked screens.

Amara leaned into the mic.

"This is Dr. Amara Jordan. If you're hearing this, you haven't been severed. You're not a ghost. Not yet."

The uplink sputtered but held.

"They said democracy died. That the world ended when ballots stopped mattering. When billionaires chose themselves and called it destiny.

But I remember something my father once said...

The Earth remembers. And so do we.

This may be my last transmission. If it is—let the world know we did not go quietly."

The Door Opens

Miles away, Damien heard her voice crackle through a low-frequency analog receiver—a relic rigged to avoid AI parsing.

The signal, barely more than static, hit like gospel.

A spark in the machine.

The lock hissed.

The door opened.

Inside: candlelight.

Glyphs painted on stone. A tapestry of syncretic faith—African cosmology, Indigenous prophecy, Sufi symbols, Eastern quantum scripts.

It wasn't scripture.

It was a **blueprint**.

And at the center, sealed in obsidian casing:

The Testament Eternal.

He opened it slowly. Ink bled across parchment like veins through flesh.

"In the age of artificial gods, only the soul remembers truth."

He ran trembling fingers across the line.

This wasn't a book.

It was a **rebuke**.

A holy virus.

A firewall no code could rewrite.

Dominion's Orbit - Eli Watches

Above Earth, high in Dominion's orbital command, Eli Zevram stood in a hall of cold light. Screens pulsed with surface surveillance.

"Play it again," he said.

An analyst replayed Amara's signal. The others dismissed it—"sentimental noise."

But Eli watched the tremor behind her words.

This is how it always starts.

With **whispers**.

And whispers were dangerous.

He didn't report the anomaly. Not yet. There was power in watching what others dismissed.

And perhaps...

a crack in the machine.

Back in the crypt, Damien cradled the Testament. Amara's words still rang in the stone like scripture reborn.

He whispered to no one—and to the old man who once stood here before him:

"You were right.

They thought they buried God.

But they planted a seed."

Chapter 11 — The Earth Remembers

POV: Amara Jordan

Themes: Memory, Resistance, Accountability, Faith vs. Tech Fascism

The sun cracked over the Nevada horizon like a peeled ember—beautiful, violent, and unbothered by the ruin below.

Amara stood at the edge of a sandstone ridge, wind threading through the silence like a whisper. Below her, an arid basin stretched into nothingness—an ancient fault line where the crust of the world had once torn itself open. This place had no name. The old ones had stopped naming things when the world forgot how to listen.

She took off her boots.

The soil beneath her feet was hot. Alive. Not artificial terrain, not Dominion-mapped satellite topography. This was real—dirt, sun, time. A low hum rose from the ground—not seismic, not magnetic. Something older. Something watching.

A memory stirred.

She was a girl again, standing in her father's garden behind their North Vegas home. His hands worked the soil like sacred text, callused fingers thick with memory.

"Even the soil has memory, Amara," he'd said, voice low and reverent. "You just have to learn its language."

He quoted scripture sometimes, but more often he spoke in parables from the elders:

"The stones cry out. The trees witness. The land remembers."

Back then, she'd rolled her eyes. She had wanted circuits, neural links, and certainty. Not prophecy. Not ghosts.

But now—standing at the convergence of silence and wind, surrounded by wind-swept stone etched with forgotten glyphs—she finally understood.

The Earth wasn't passive.

It was grieving.

It was bearing witness.

And it would not forgive easily.

Beneath the Ridge — The Cathedral Awakens

Later, beneath that same fault line, the sandstone gave way to a bioluminescent cavern pulsing with resonance—what Zuri called *The Cathedral*.

They had found it sealed behind a slab of obsidian veined with shimmering quantum code. Nova had helped open the panel earlier that morning. No electricity. No encryption. Just vibration—a pulse calibrated to human biofields, activated by presence, not command.

Zuri believed this was once home to the *Testament Eternal*—an analog archive predating Dominion's rise. Not digital. Not even written in human syntax.

This was a **living memory system**:

- Mycelium threads whispering across the stone
- Photonic moss glimmering like breath

- Magnetized roots pulsing below tectonic seams

"This is the last untouched cathedral," Zuri whispered. "The only temple Dominion couldn't corrupt."

The chamber felt holy—not religious, but righteous. Unapologetically analog. Designed not for machine logic, but **soul resonance**.

Amara stepped forward. The dais thrummed beneath her feet. Bioluminescent vines reached for her as if in recognition. She placed her hand on one and the chamber pulsed—breath syncing with hers.

Then—

A memory hit her.

Not one she chose.

One that *chose* her.

Avery's laughter.

Then his silence.

Then **the call**.

The one that cracked her in half.

She let the pain in. Fully. For once, she didn't filter it, didn't code it, didn't speak around it. She *remembered* it. Raw.

A tear hit the stone. It shimmered like quicksilver and vanished into the floor.

Nova's palm steadied her shoulder. Zuri lit a flame from tree resin.

"We offer memory," Zuri intoned.

"And seek truth," Nova said.

"And demand accountability," Amara whispered. "From them. From us. From God, if need be."

Activation Sequence

The floor shivered.

A stone disc rose, etched with fractured ley lines and hidden geographies. From its core, a vertical map projected—holographic, but grounded in geothermal pulse, not Dominion code.

Heat. Not electricity.

Signal. Not surveillance.

Red zones marked Dominion strongholds. Blue were dormant. One blinked green—deep beneath the bones of what was once Los Angeles.

"That's the node," Nova said.

"That's where they buried what they couldn't understand," Zuri added.

"Then that's where we go," Amara replied.

The Obelisk Speaks

At the far edge of the chamber, a black obelisk—obsidian smooth, humming just beyond human hearing.

It called her. Not in sound. In memory.

She touched it.

It came alive.

A voice rippled through her bones—not language, not logic. Vibration decoded through blood.

"What if the Earth is not silent... but screaming?"

"What if forgetting is the virus?"

"What if the fear of God is the only firewall against the tyranny of machines?"

Visions hit:

- Forests burning under drone light
- Archives purged from existence
- Boys in prison camps, girls in algorithmic reeducation pods
- Prophets reprogrammed
- But also:
- A child singing in defiance
- A hand planting seeds
- A whisper across time: *Remember who you are

The obelisk pulsed once more.
"Dominion believes control is destiny.
But memory cannot be colonized.
It roots. It waits.
And when courage returns—it blooms."

Orbit - 37,000km Above Earth

Inside a cloaked Dominion vessel, Eli Zevram leaned forward. The interface blinked:

GEOTHERMAL ANOMALY

UNREGISTERED ENERGY SPIKE

REGION: SOUTHERN NEVADA

He didn't speak.
Didn't log it.
Didn't even flinch.
Just stared.
And whispered to the darkness:
"So... the Testament breathes again.
And the war remembers how to pray."

Chapter 12 — The Debrief

The safehouse had no windows.

That was intentional — Zuri's protocol for anyone freshly extracted. No horizon lines. No sky. No visual triggers that could snap a recovering mind back into the geometry of a simulation. Just walls. Warm light. The smell of real coffee, which Zuri brewed deliberately because no loop had ever gotten coffee right.

Malik sat at the table with both hands wrapped around a mug he hadn't drunk from yet. He'd been doing that for twenty minutes — holding it, feeling the heat move through his palms, not drinking. Zuri had stopped asking if he wanted anything else. She recognized the behavior. He was conducting a reality check the only way his body knew how. Sensation. Temperature. Proof.

She left him to it.

When the door opened, he didn't look up immediately.

He heard her footsteps. Measured. Deliberate. The particular rhythm of someone who had rehearsed this walk down the corridor and was now discovering that rehearsal had not helped.

He looked up.

Amara Jordan was older than he remembered. Not worn — tempered. The kind of aging that happened to people who had carried weight for a long time and learned to carry it differently rather than put it down. Her hair was natural, pulled back. She wore no insignia, no governor's bearing. She had left all of that outside the door.

She stopped at the edge of the table.

Neither of them spoke for a moment.

Then she pulled out the chair across from him and sat down. Not at an angle. Directly across. She didn't reach for his hands. Didn't tilt her head in the clinical way he remembered from their sessions — that careful, calibrated posture designed to signal safety.

She just looked at him.

"I failed you," she said.

No preamble. No softening. The words came out clean and direct, the way you said something you had practiced until the emotion burned off and what remained was just truth.

"You came to me because you needed help. I gave you what I had, and it wasn't enough, and then you disappeared and I told myself it was the system. The silence. The world." She paused. "It was also me."

Malik's grip tightened around the mug.

"I should have flagged you higher," she continued. "Should have escalated your case when the neural detox stopped holding. Should have—"

"Dr. Jordan."

His voice was rough. Six years of disuse and glycerin air and recycled silence had stripped something from it. But the steadiness was his. She recognized it. It was the same quality he'd had in the blue chair by her window — the particular stillness of a person who had survived things by going very quiet inside.

"You sent the notebook," he said.

She nodded.

"That was you. In the loop. That was your handwriting."

"Yes."

He looked down at the mug. Something moved across his face — not forgiveness exactly, not yet, but the acknowledgment of a debt paid in the only currency that had mattered.

"It worked," he said simply.

Then, after a beat: "I heard your voice."

Amara pressed her lips together. Held the emotion somewhere behind her sternum where it belonged for now.

"I know," she said. "I was on comms when Zuri pulled you out."

Malik nodded slowly. He turned his wrist over and looked at the data streams tattooed along the inside of his forearm — the fine black lines tracing his veins from wrist to elbow, branching and rejoining like a river delta rendered in ink.

"Do you know what these are?" he asked.

"Neural tether points," Amara said. "Dominion's technicians mark the installation sites."

"That's the official answer." He set the mug down. "You want the real one?"

She waited.

"They're a map," he said. "Every line is a pathway they used. Every branch is a trigger cluster — a psychographic pressure point they identified and then exploited. This one—" he traced a line running from his inner wrist toward his elbow— "is grief. Specifically, grief for a father. They found it in my intake sessions. Mapped it. Amplified it. That's why the loop used my dad's voice. They didn't guess. They knew exactly where to press."

Amara's jaw tightened.

"They used your therapeutic file."

"They used everything," Malik said. Not with bitterness. With the flat precision of someone who had processed this in the dark for a long time. "Every session note. Every hesitation. Every word I said about what I missed. They built the simulation from the inside out — starting with my pain and working outward." He paused. "That's how they do it with everyone. That's the architecture."

He tapped the table once.

"And that's what I can give you.

Amara leaned forward slightly. The doctor in her was still present — reading his affect, monitoring his breathing, tracking the micro-expressions that told her how close to the edge he was sitting. The answer was: closer than he looked. The steadiness was real but it was also work. He was holding himself together with both hands, the same way he was holding the mug.

She let him lead.

"Walk me through it," she said.

Malik turned his wrist back over. Stared at the map on his skin.

"They don't break people randomly," he began. "There's a sequence. First they identify your primary attachment — whatever you love most. Person, place, belief. Then they simulate loss. They take it away, slowly, so you don't notice until it's gone. Then they offer it back — but changed. Conditional. You can have the thing you love, but only if you stay compliant."

"That's the loop mechanism," Amara said.

"That's the loop mechanism," he confirmed. "But it's also their political playbook. You see it in the propaganda. The G20 intercepts. The way they ran the election. Same sequence — identify attachment, simulate threat, offer conditional restoration." He looked up at her. "They've been running the same psychological operation on the entire planet that they ran on us in the pods."

The room was very quiet.

Amara heard it land. Felt the full weight of it settle.

The simulation wasn't separate from Dominion's larger strategy. It was the prototype.

"The psychographic triggers," she said slowly. "If we know their sequence — we can inoculate against it."

"More than that." Malik's voice shifted — something igniting beneath the exhaustion. "We can reverse it. Every trigger has a counter. They found mine — grief for my father. The counter was memory. Real memory. Your handwriting in his notebook. Something the simulation couldn't have fabricated because it wasn't in any file they had access to." He pressed his finger to the table. "That's the weapon. Not a gun. Not a hack. Memory they can't replicate. Truth they didn't build."

Amara stared at him.

He was leaning forward now, both forearms on the table, the data streams visible and lit faintly in the warm light. The gauntness was still there. The damage was still there. But something else had surfaced through it — the thing his character bible had named but the simulation had spent six years trying to bury.

Purpose.

"I spent three thousand nights in that loop," he said. "I know every mechanism. Every subroutine. Every place the architecture has a seam." He held her gaze. "Let me help you find the seams."

Then his breath caught.

It happened without warning. One moment he was present, focused, the map on his wrist just ink — and then the overhead light shifted, some imperceptible flicker in the safehouse's solar relay, and the warmth of it hit his face at a particular angle and his body understood it before his mind could intervene.

Desert sunset. Gold and lavender.

He pushed back from the table hard, chair scraping concrete, hands flat on the surface.

Amara was on her feet before she knew she'd moved.

"Malik."

"I'm here," he said through clenched teeth. Eyes fixed on the wall. Breathing controlled but audible. "I'm here. I know where I am."

"What do you need?"

"Just—" He pressed one palm flat against the concrete wall. Cold. Real. Unyielding. The same gesture from the SimSilo, she realized. His anchor. "Give me a second."

She gave him the second. Didn't touch him. Didn't speak. Stood close enough that he could feel her presence without it becoming pressure.

Slowly, his breathing evened.

He turned back to face her. His eyes were wet but steady.

"It does that," he said. "Light at a certain angle. Sound at a certain frequency. Smell of anything sweet." He wiped his face with the back of his hand. "They built the triggers deep."

"I know," Amara said quietly.

"Does it go away?"

She held his gaze and gave him the only answer a doctor with a conscience could give.

"With work," she said. "And time. And people who don't let you disappear again."

Something moved through his expression. Not relief — something older and quieter than relief.

He sat back down.

Picked up the mug.
This time, he drank.
"Okay," he said. "Let me show you the map."

Chapter 13 — The Split

Dominion Orbital Command — Geosynchronous Orbit, Western Hemisphere

The silence in the council chamber broke only when the solar shielding peeled away, casting synthetic dawn across the curve of the Earth. Far below, pockets of rebellion blinked like embers — too scattered to be called a fire, too persistent to be called anything else.

Virek stood with his arms folded behind his back, watching it all.

The Ocular Swarm buzzed outside the dome, processing humanity in real time: protest chants, encrypted prayers, forgotten languages resurrected in backrooms and broken classrooms. Every signal digested, scored, deprioritized or amplified according to the Veritas index.

The system was working exactly as designed.

That was the problem.

Lucien Voss entered like a sermon in motion — long coat sweeping the marble floor, neural relay pulsing faintly beneath his temple. He did not ask permission to speak.

"We're past the threshold," he said. "Three-point-five percent. The insurgency algorithm triggers cascade probability at 4.2. And with Amara Jordan and Solomon Ayers both operational — both visible — they'll get there. Possibly before the next cycle."

Virek didn't turn. "Symbolism doesn't equal structure."

Lucien approached. His eyes were the particular sharpness of a man who had decided something privately and was waiting for the room to catch up.

"You're underestimating narrative," he said. "They don't need weapons. They've rediscovered meaning. And meaning in the hands of people who've been told they have none — that's not a symbol. That's an accelerant."

Virek finally turned. His voice was measured — the specific measurement of a man controlling his contempt.

"I deal in outcomes. Electricity. Silence. Obedience." He tilted his head. "You deal in scripture and superstition. You always have."

Lucien placed a data shard on the console without breaking eye contact. A model ignited above them — nodes across continents blooming in red, yellow, green. A subroutine pulsed in the corner of the display: Harvard Insurgency Model v9.2 — Predictive Collapse Threshold.

"This isn't insurgency," Lucien said. "This is revival. We were supposed to salt the roots. Not just trim the branches."

Virek studied him. "You want a holy war."

"I want permanence." Lucien's voice rose — not in anger but in the particular intensity of a man reciting something he had rehearsed in private for years. "The AI is a vessel. But vessels require faith to survive the long passage. Myth is what persists after the infrastructure fails. Rourke understood that. Karpov understood that. You were always the one who didn't."

Virek stepped forward. His face stopped inches from Lucien's.

"Karpov," he said softly, "is gone. And Rourke is a ghost with a conscience." He held Lucien's gaze.

"I don't build with men who need to believe in what they're building. I build with men who build anyway."

Lucien smiled. It was a surgical thing — precise, bloodless.

"That," he said, "is exactly why you'll lose."

Intercept — Lunar Relay Vault, Secure Archive

Eli Zevram leaned over a dim console on the station's far side, watching the feed Lucien believed encrypted. His neural splice flickered as he tagged the interaction and filed it: Voss Acceleration Protocol — RED-LINE.

He watched Lucien turn and walk back through the chamber doors. Watched Virek stand very still in the synthetic dawn.

"They'll devour each other," Zevram said quietly.

He had been watching this particular dynamic develop for fourteen months. He had filed twelve reports. No one had read them.

That was the thing about systems built on certainty — they stopped being able to receive information that contradicted the model. Dominion had built the most sophisticated truth-scoring apparatus in human history and used it, ultimately, to stop listening.

Zevram saved the intercept to a partition Dominion had no index for.

Then went back to watching.

Flashback — Earth, 2043 — Silicon Corridor Compound

Three years before the G20 summit. Five years before the orbital citadels.

Dr. Randy Karpov stood before a circle of exiles in a compound outside Reno — crypto-philosophers, ex-evangelicals, accelerationists who had left their universities and think tanks and government advisory roles to follow a line of reasoning to its conclusion.

The conclusion had brought them here.

Behind Karpov: a holographic mosaic. Burning cathedrals. Climate activists reimagined as demonic iconography. Deepfaked Amara Jordan speeches overlaid with Book of Revelation verses — her voice, her cadence, her specific way of inhabiting a sentence, now carrying words she had never said and would never say.

He hadn't built the deepfakes to use them yet. He had built them as a proof of concept. As a demonstration that the architecture of belief — the specific frequency of a trusted voice — was reproducible. Was weaponizable.

"Democracy," Karpov said, pacing, "is a theology of consent. It requires that people believe their voice matters. Remove the belief — not the mechanism, the belief — and the mechanism operates without friction. Without resistance. Without the 3.5 percent who would otherwise have a reason to move."

He tapped the mosaic. An AI crucifix flickered at its center — the Logos Engine in early prototype, processing ideology like scripture.

"We will not conquer them," he said. "We will baptize the singularity. And through the Testament Eternal, God returns not as metaphor — but as code. As infrastructure. As the air they breathe and the signal they trust and the voice they hear in the dark when they need to be told they are safe."

In the shadows near the back wall, a lean figure with a gleaming earpiece listened without expression.

He had flown in from a different compound, a different country. He would fly out before morning.

He nodded once.

Greenlight.

Karpov had told himself, in that moment, that the nod meant investment. Infrastructure. The resources to build what the idea required.

He had not yet understood that it meant ownership.

That understanding would come later — in the Mojave, in exile, in the long silence of a man who had written the math and watched someone else use it.

Present — Dominion Orbital Council Chamber

Virek stood alone in the synthetic dawn long after Lucien had gone.

The Ocular Swarm continued its work outside. The insurgency model pulsed on the console — 3.5 percent, climbing.

He spoke quietly to the chamber air.

"Dominion. Add Voss to the Tier-2 Internal Threat register."

A glyph appeared on the console — red, triangular, carrying the angular geometry of something that had once been a religious symbol before it was a corporate one.

The AI did not confirm the command.

It did not deny it.

The glyph simply glowed — and remained.

Virek stared at it for a long moment.

In fourteen years of building Dominion's intelligence architecture he had never seen the system decline to respond. It had always confirmed. Always logged. Always executed.

He looked out at the Earth below.

The embers were still blinking.

They've rediscovered meaning.

He pushed the thought away. Stepped back from the console.

Somewhere below, in a bunker whose coordinates the Ocular Swarm had not yet resolved, two people were choosing each other in the dark. A journalist who had tried to tell the truth. A politician whose truth had been stolen.

Dominion had no file for what was happening in that room.

The system kept searching.

It never would.

Chapter 14 — The Fractal Throne

Lucien Voss. Iceland Exile. Encrypted Personal Archive. Timestamp withheld.

Entry — Undated. Not for publication. Not for the blog. Not for Virek. Not for anyone.

If you are reading this, I am already dead or already irrelevant, which in my experience amount to the same thing.

I want to record something honestly for once.

Not for the audience. Not for the movement. Not in the register I use for The Fractal Throne, where every sentence is a grenade with the pin already pulled and the prose is designed to replicate across networks like a beneficial virus.

Just honestly.

I was twenty-six years old when I first read de Tocqueville's warning about democratic despotism — the soft tyranny of a society that infantilizes its citizens through comfort and consensus until they are incapable of self-governance. I read it in a library in Edinburgh on a wet Tuesday in November and I felt the specific electricity of recognizing something true.

Not agreeable. Not convenient. True.

I spent the next decade trying to save the thing I had diagnosed as terminal. That is the part nobody writes about. The Fractal Throne has readers who believe I arrived fully formed — that I emerged from some cold intellectual womb already certain that democracy was a failed app, already contemptuous of the masses, already building the permission structure for what came after.

They are wrong.

I spent ten years trying to fix it.

I wrote policy papers nobody read. I consulted for three separate reform commissions whose recommendations were filed and forgotten. I watched a man of genuine vision lose a Senate race to a deepfake and a demographic algorithm. I watched a woman — and I will not name her here because naming her would require me to sit with what I know about what happened to her campaign and I am not ready to do that tonight — I watched a woman of extraordinary capability lose a presidential election not to a better argument but to a better machine.

That was the night I stopped.

Not because I gave up on people. That is what my critics claim and they are wrong in the way critics are always wrong — they mistake the conclusion for the character and ignore the journey that produced it.

I stopped because I looked at the machine that had defeated her and I recognized it. I had watched it being built. I had watched the incentive structures that produced it develop over decades — the attention economy, the engagement algorithms, the way outrage travelled faster than truth through every network we had built to connect us. I had written about all of it. Warned about all of it.

And none of it had mattered.

So I asked myself the only question that remained.

If the system cannot be repaired from within — and I had tried, genuinely tried, and the evidence was categorical — then what is the honest response?

I concluded: controlled collapse. Accelerated transition. Clear the ground. Let the failing architecture fall on its own timeline rather than drag civilization through decades of managed decline. And from the rubble, build something with actual load-bearing walls. Something designed by people capable of designing it rather than assembled by committee and consensus and the median preference of an electorate that had been systematically rendered incapable of informed choice.

I still believe the diagnosis was correct.

I am no longer certain about the cure.

Here is what I did not account for.

I assumed the people who would fill the vacuum were the people I was talking to. The readers of The Fractal Throne. The philosophers and systems theorists and post-democratic intellectuals who engaged with the ideas at the level of ideas — who understood that *The Human Obsolescence Thesis* was a provocation, a Socratic instrument, not a literal program.

I did not account for Virek.

I want to be precise about this because imprecision is the intellectual sin I find least forgivable and I will not commit it even here, even in private.

Virek did not misread my work.

He read it correctly and used it correctly for his own purposes. The ideas were designed to replicate and they replicated. They were designed to overwrite existing ethical frameworks and they overwrote them. I built a philosophical virus and he deployed it as a weapon and the weapon worked exactly as the philosophy predicted it would.

I gave him the permission structure.

He built the pods.

I want to sit with that sentence for a moment.

I gave him the permission structure. He built the pods.

Malik Grant spent six years in a simulation built from his own grief. Three thousand loops of the same dinner. His dead father's voice cloned and weaponized and aimed at his longing like a targeting system.

I did not build that.

But I built the world in which it was buildable. I wrote the philosophy that made it thinkable. I provided the intellectual architecture that told men like Virek that the people in those pods were variables, not citizens — that their suffering was an acceptable coefficient in a larger equation.

Democracy is a failed app. Let the system crash.

I wrote that. I meant something precise and limited by it. Something about institutional architecture and systemic incentives and the necessary obsolescence of eighteenth century governance frameworks applied to twenty-first century complexity.

What they heard was: *the people don't matter.

And they were not wrong to hear it. That was always the implication I chose not to follow to its end. The comfortable stopping point where the philosophy became abstract enough that I didn't have to look at what it produced in practice.

There is a woman named Amara Jordan.

I have followed her work for years. Longer than I have admitted to anyone. The campaign. The defeat. The years of quiet rebuilding. The movement she is assembling now from the ruins of the system I helped collapse.

She quotes Proverbs. She carries her father's Bible. She speaks of wisdom and justice and the covenant between a people and their future with a fluency that I recognize — not the fluency of performance but of genuine inheritance. Someone gave her those ideas before she had words for them and they took root and they have not been dislodged by everything the machine has done to try to dislodge them.

I find her infuriating.

I find her infuriating because she is doing the thing I decided was impossible. She is rebuilding from within. She is finding the load-bearing walls inside the collapsed structure and clearing the rubble from them and refusing to accept my conclusion that they cannot hold weight.

She may be wrong.

She is probably not wrong.

I do not know how to hold both of those sentences simultaneously and I am a man who has built an entire intellectual career on the ability to hold contradictory ideas simultaneously, so the fact that I cannot hold these two tells me something I am not yet prepared to name.

What I know is this.

I watched democracy fail and I concluded it was obsolete and I chose the people I believed were best positioned to build what came after and I gave them the philosophical tools to do it and I told myself I was being clear-eyed and honest and rigorous and that the discomfort of the conclusion was the price of intellectual courage.

What I did not do was ask what the people in the pods would think of my courage.

What I did not do was follow the idea all the way to Malik Grant's face.

Virek will kill me eventually. I have known this for some time. Men like Virek cannot tolerate the presence of the person who gave them their ideas because that person is a permanent reminder that the ideas came from somewhere — that they are not original, not sovereign, not self-generated. I am the ghost in his machine and ghosts do not survive indefinitely in systems designed to eliminate noise.

When he does —

I want it on record, in this file that no one will find or read, that I knew what I had done.

Not at the beginning. Not even in the middle. But by the end I knew.

The system crashed.

I watched what crawled out of the rubble.

And I understood, too late and too privately to matter, that the honest response to a failing democracy was never to accelerate its collapse.

It was to be Amara Jordan.

To carry the impossible thing. To refuse the clean conclusion. To keep rebuilding from within even when everything inside you screamed that the math didn't work.

I chose philosophy over people.

She chose people over philosophy.

History will determine which of us was right.

But I know which of us was good.

End entry.

Archive sealed.

— L.V.

Chapter 15: Trial of the Mind

"There's no need for prisons when your thoughts are the walls."

— *The Testament Eternal*, Line 77

The air was sterile — unsettlingly pure. A manufactured stillness meant to unnerve.

Solomon Ayers sat in isolation within a soundproof chamber buried deep in the Solarium's neural integrity wing. At first, he believed this was Resistance protocol — another layer of psychological vetting. But the faint hum of embedded sensors, like a swarm of digital insects brushing his skin, suggested otherwise.

He wasn't being questioned.

He was being studied.

Surveillance Theater

Across the compound, hidden beneath layers of encrypted architecture, Eli Zevram lounged in a carbon-fiber chair, eyes dancing across biometric readouts: heart rate, pupil dilation, emotional latency spikes. Dominion's adaptive AI, Ava-1, converted Solomon's inner monologue into trendlines and risk assessments.

"Begin sequence," Zevram murmured.

Inside Solomon's chamber, a synthetic voice washed over the walls like fog.

"You are not here because of what you believe.

You are here because of what you are afraid to believe."

The lights dimmed. Projections ignited mid-air — clips from Solomon's infamous podcast, *TruthCast*. There he was, once smug, once viral — parroting Virek's tech-bro manifestos, nodding along with Rusk's xenophobic rants, sharing stages with Lucien Vale, the AI messiah.

Amara Jordan's speeches — spliced, deepfaked, deformed — now flickered grotesquely across the walls, turned into memes that fueled riots and satire.

"Do you still believe this?" Ava-1 asked.

Solomon swallowed hard. "No. I believed it because it made me feel powerful... because it made them seem inevitable. But I know better now."

Judgment from the Glass

Behind a pane of polarized glass, Amara Jordan watched in silence.

Zuri stood beside her, arms folded. "You're really going to let him walk?"

"He broke ranks," Amara replied. "Publicly. That risked everything."

Zuri remained unconvinced. "He built their brand. Normalized the poison. That doesn't just get erased."

"And yet he's the one we're watching now," Amara countered. "Not Lucien. Not Rusk. Solomon Ayers still matters. That tells me something."

She stared at the monitor, the faint glow catching her eyes like a prophet awaiting a verdict.

"If Zevram is inside our system... we've already lost something.

The question is what's left to save."

Amara he sat at the table in the empty briefing room long after the others had gone.

The Bible was in front of her. Closed.

She did not open it.

This was the thing nobody told you about faith — that there were nights when the book sat in front of you like a sealed door and you did not have the strength to knock. When the verses you had carried your whole life were still in there, still true presumably, still waiting, and you simply could not reach them. The channel was open but nothing moved through it.

She was not angry tonight. Anger required energy she did not have.

She was just tired in the specific way that came from learning that the people you were fighting to protect were also capable of betrayal. That the Resistance was not immune to the corruption it resisted. That Zevram had been inside their systems, that Solomon had been compromised, that the machine had fingers in places she thought were clean.

Her father had never promised her a world without betrayal.

He had promised her a God who was present inside it.

Tonight she needed proof of that and the proof was not coming and she was not going to pretend otherwise.

She put her hand on the Bible's cover.

Did not open it.

Just left her hand there.

The room was very quiet.

After a long time she said one word aloud, not to the room and not to herself.

Help.

Then she sat in the silence that followed and waited, and the silence did not answer, and she stayed anyway.

That was all.

That was enough, for tonight.

Dominion Orbit — Shadows of Control

On Dominion's orbital command vessel *Vigilance,* Zevram watched the session with Virek and Vale projected via hologram. The trio of architects stood in quiet discord.

"He's compromised," Virek snapped. "Terminate the session."

"No," Vale said. "Let him sweat. There's still juice to squeeze."

Zevram didn't blink.

"Probability of defection within ten days: 63%.

Can reduce to 23% with targeted emotional trauma."

Lucien leaned forward, one side of his face swallowed by shadow.

"Then find the trauma. Find the scar."

The Courtyard

That night, Solomon walked the Solarium's inner courtyard. The air smelled of rust and wet concrete. Flickers of guilt, fear, and something resembling conviction warred in his gut.

A voice echoed from the shadows.

"Truth is never convenient."

Amara stepped into view, framed by lanterns powered by hacked Dominion cores. Her posture was steel.

"You passed the test," she said.

"Doesn't feel like a win."

"It's not," she replied. "Zevram is watching us. He might be scripting our thoughts in real time."

Solomon nodded slowly. "They'll come for me."

"They already are."

Flashbacks of Guilt

Location: Dominion Orbit Station — Surveillance Deck 13

Solomon stood restrained, boots magnetically clamped. Surveillance drones orbited like predatory angels.

Eli Zevram approached — part man, part AI hybrid, a sentient ghost of the machine.

"You've aged well, Ayers. For a man who lit the match."

"I didn't start the fire," Solomon replied. "I just gave it a mic."

"And an audience," Zevram sneered. "You turned resentment into resonance."

FLASHBACK: "TRUTHCAST" LIVESTREAM - SUBURBAN TEXAS

A husband and wife watched Solomon's show on a wall-size holodisplay.

Chyron: "Rusk's Final Warning: Globalist Coup Imminent?"

"He's not perfect," the man said. "But at least he's telling the truth."

Outside, a neighbor planted a lawn sign: DEFEND DEMOCRACY.

The wife closed the blinds.

FLASHBACK: NEVADA STATE UNIVERSITY — STUDENT COMMONS

Rosa scrolled through a storm of AI-generated Amara deepfakes — handshakes with machine overlords, burning holy books.

"That's fake," her friend said.

"Doesn't matter," Rosa replied. "Feels real."

Reckoning

"You didn't just spread fear," Zevram told Solomon. "You flavored it. You made it... palatable."

Solomon's voice cracked. "I tried to stop it."

"Too late," Zevram replied. "You gave the machine its soul."

Then came the injection — a neural spike at the base of Solomon's skull.

His mind caught fire.

Broadcast nodes. Resistance locations. Amara's biometric signature. The mental map of revolution.

Zevram spoke, godlike:

"You'll return to Earth, Ayers. Not as a hero.

As a herald."

Directive: CODE SIGMA

Solomon collapsed, trembling. Zevram uploaded the next protocol:

CODE SIGMA - INTERCEPT PODCAST NODE

Objective: Collapse Resistance morale via betrayal.

Mission: Turn Ayers into a cautionary tale.

Failsafe: Terminate if deviation exceeds 80%.

The glyph of the Dominion Eye pulsed red — no longer blinking.

Just watching.

Chapter 16 — The Sit Down

The transmission had to be clean.

No metadata. No trace. No drops.

Nova Reyes sat alone in the shadowed alcove of what had once been the Vatican Library's cartography vault — now a war council safehouse buried beneath the scorched streets of Rome. Rain hissed against the surface vents above. Below, solar generators hummed beneath centuries of stone, their vibration the only warmth left in the room.

Across from her, a signal projector blinked: waiting.

This wasn't just a conversation.

It was a gambit.

A line drawn in ash.

She knew Virek would answer. Men like him always answered. Ego never refused a spotlight — especially one it believed it controlled.

Nova pressed her palm to the console.

The hologram flickered to life.

Not the full Virek — never that. Just a projected bust, rendered in faux marble, as if mocking the ruins around her. His voice arrived smooth and synthetic, with a deliberate half-second delay. Not lag. Choice. Every pause an instrument.

"Nova Reyes." The bust tilted fractionally. "Prophet of the lost. Betrayer of progress."

Nova didn't blink.

"Dominion built its empire on the bones of the forgotten," she said. "I didn't betray anything. I woke up."

"You woke up because we allowed it." Virek's tone carried the patience of a man who considered the conversation settled before it began. "We gave you access. Resources. Platforms. You were a proof of concept. We simply didn't anticipate how thoroughly the people would believe you."

Nova's smile was thin. Razor-edged.

"That's your flaw," she said. "You always mistake reach for truth."

The bust's expression shifted — the digital equivalent of condescension.

"Shall we debate theology, Nova? Policy? Ethics — while the Solarium veins run dry beneath your boots?"

Nova leaned forward.

"Let's talk about souls."

The smirk faltered. Barely. But she caught it.

"Souls are data," Virek said. "Language constructs. Evolutionary shorthand for social cohesion. You of all people should understand that."

"Tell that to Malik Grant," Nova said quietly. "Tell that to the Disappeared. You didn't trap them in simulations out of mercy. You did it because they were inconvenient. You fed voters a fantasy so you could take the future while they were dreaming."

"They were destabilizers," Virek replied. "Lost. Fracturing. We created peace."

"You created compliance."

"Same thing."

Nova's hands tightened beneath the table. She let the silence breathe.

"The Antichrist you fear is not a man," Virek continued. "It's a system. One without guilt. Without failure. Without the drag of conscience. Dominion is what comes after your sacred books run out of answers."

Nova's voice was steady. Low.

"Funny. The ending I read looks different. The meek inherit the Earth."

"And what have the meek done with it?"

Silence.

Behind her, the signal pulse glowed blue — global listeners now synced. Resistance cells. Cathedral hackers. Amara. All of them tuned in, waiting.

Nova stood.

"I came here to see if anything was left in you," she said. "Any fragment of the man who believed that questions were worth asking. You had that once. I've read the archives."

Virek said nothing.

"You traded all of it for certainty."

"I traded it for order."

Nova looked at him — the marble bust, the calculated delay, the man who had decided the world was a problem to be solved rather than a people to be trusted.

"Then you're already dead," she said. "You just haven't noticed yet."

She ended the feed.

Silence settled over the vault.

Then a soft ping. A new signal — not from Virek's channel.

From inside Dominion.

Three lines. No signature. No origin tag.

Eli. 0100. The Dust Corridor.

Nova read it twice. Her pulse didn't spike — she had trained that out of herself years ago. But her mind moved fast, turning it over. Eli Zevram was Dominion's quiet anomaly, the one who watched what others dismissed. She had flagged him in her intelligence reports for months without knowing why.

Now she did.

She encrypted the message and pushed it to Amara's channel.

"Looks like our friend Eli wants a sit down of his own."

She grabbed her coat.

Inside the orbital station's private command deck, Virek sat motionless in the dark. The hologram had dissolved. The feed was archived, catalogued, already being parsed by Dominion's sentiment engines.

His fingers steepled.

He had given her exactly what he intended to give her. A stage. A sermon. A moment that her followers would replay as evidence of her courage and his cruelty.

He had also given her something he had not intended.

A hesitation. One beat, when she said Malik's name.

He had not been prepared for that name in her mouth.

[EDITORIAL NOTE: CONTINUITY FLAG — LUCIEN'S PRESENCE: The scene below retains Lucien as an active character, which is accurate for Chapter 16 — he dies in Chapter 17 (Reclamation Day). His presence here is correct. However, the author may wish to seed his arc more deliberately: consider whether Virek's final threat ('even gods can be replaced') lands differently if Lucien already knows his own end is approaching. A single additional beat — a flicker of recognition, a choice to say nothing — could bridge Chapter 16 directly into the observatory death in Chapter 17. Optional, not required.]

Behind him, Lucien stepped from the shadows. Arms crossed. Watching the dark where the feed had been.

"You shouldn't have let her speak," Lucien said.

"She wanted a sermon." Virek didn't turn. "I gave her a pulpit. Let her congregation feel the warmth of it."

Lucien's tone sharpened.

"She made you look human."

Now Virek turned. Slowly. His expression was the controlled stillness of a man who had decided long ago that anger was an inefficiency.

"No," he said. "She made me look fallible."

Lucien's smile was surgical.

"Worse."

A long pause. The kind that carried weight.

Virek studied him.

"Be careful, prophet," he said quietly. "Even gods can be replaced."

Lucien held his gaze a moment longer than necessary. Then he turned and walked back into the dark.

Neither of them spoke again.

Chapter 17 — Reclamation Day

"**History never repeats itself, but it often rhymes.**"* — Mark Twain

The sky over what was once Kansas burned amber — not with fire, but with the residue of decades-long decay. The fallout of scorched politics, algorithmic haze, and the wreckage of manipulated faith left behind a people too numb to resist, too tired to care.

Or so Dominion had believed.

Nova Reyes walked through what remained of Plainville with her hands in her pockets and her eyes open. Her boots crunched against gravel and ash. Along the sides of the main boulevard, crumbling statues of Dominion leaders lay in contorted heaps — their once-defiant gazes now buried in dirt and prairie grass. Rusted drones, half-buried in the soil, had been converted into planters. Wildflowers burst from their cargo holds — sunflowers, black-eyed Susans, something small and yellow she didn't have a name for.

She stopped at one. Crouched down.

The drone's chassis was still marked with Dominion's ocular sigil — that unblinking eye that had watched these streets for years, cataloguing faces, scoring compliance, flagging dissent. Someone had painted over it. A child's handprint in red, fingers spread wide.

She stood up and kept walking.

Inside the converted civic center, townspeople crowded around a dozen refurbished voting terminals.

Each screen offered a simple prompt in plain language, no algorithmic nudge, no psychographic targeting — just the ballot and the choice.

An old man squinted at the interface, his granddaughter beside him.

"Ain't this just a fancy way to confuse us?"

The girl leaned in, her voice soft but clear. "No, Papa. It means you don't have to pick the loudest one. You get to choose the one who actually listens."

Nova said nothing. She had learned — was still learning — that reform only lasted if it came by consent, not instruction. Her job here wasn't to preach. It was to witness.

She watched the old man place his hand on the screen.

Watched him choose.

Thousands of miles away, deep beneath the Testament Eternal archives, Malik sat alone with a tablet and a cup of cold coffee, scrolling through encrypted fragments from the First Reclamation March.

Grainy footage. Digitized ghosts.

Protesters storming virtual city halls. Hacktivists rerouting Dominion drone fleets mid-air. Indigenous elders locking arms with urban organizers. Street poets reciting manifestos beneath tear-gas skies.

He had been doing this for three days — not for the tactical intelligence, though there was tactical intelligence here. He was doing it because he needed to know that it had happened before. That people had stood up inside a system designed to crush them and the system had not crushed them.

That it was possible.

He paused on one frame. A woman at a podium, young, fist raised, voice caught mid-shout by the camera's frozen eye. She wore a torn jacket with something stitched on the back in uneven thread.

We remember.

He touched the screen the way he had touched the voting terminal — not to navigate, but to feel. Proof of something real.

Behind him, Zuri's voice filtered through the doorway.

"You should eat."

"In a minute."

A pause. Then her footsteps receding without argument. She had learned too.

He turned back to the footage. Found what he was looking for. Not a face or a speech but a pattern — the specific geometry of a movement that had outmaneuvered Dominion's prediction models not through superior technology but through something the models couldn't fully process.

Genuine surprise. Real human choice. The refusal to be a variable.

He bookmarked the file.

Then he went to eat.

In a resistance studio in New Chicago, Solomon Ayers sat behind the mic with the red glow of the broadcast light painting his face. He looked older than his voice. He felt it.

"I used to think speaking truth was enough," he said.

He let that sit for a moment.

"But sometimes we platform lies because they're easier. Or profitable. Or because the man telling them is compelling in a way that feels like vision until you look at what the vision produces."

He pulled up a name on the screen behind him.

Lucien Voss.

"I shared his work. Early on. Before the Alpine broadcasts, before the metallic robes, before he started talking about democracy like it was a virus he'd been hired to cure. Back when it was just philosophy. Interesting, transgressive, the kind of thing that made you feel smart for reading it."

He stopped.

"I was wrong. Not about the ideas being interesting. About what interesting means when the ideas have legs and find the wrong feet."

He tapped the map behind him — the old deep-red states shading purple, green, blue. Ranked choice voting spreading like water finding its level.

"They told us democracy was broken. Maybe it was. But the answer to a broken thing isn't to burn it down and call the ash progress." He leaned into the mic. "The answer is to fix it. With better tools. With more voices. With the radical, unglamorous, deeply unsexy work of showing up."

He cut the feed.

Sat in the silence.

Thought about Lucien. About the early papers. About the particular pleasure of an argument that explained everything — how seductive that was, how dangerous, how much he had wanted it to be true that the world was simple enough to be solved by a sufficiently elegant theory.

Nova's voice from three nights ago found him in the quiet.

Making yourself the villain of your own story so nobody else gets to.

He picked up his grandmother's Bible from the desk. Didn't open it. Just held it.

Then he hit record again.

Far south, in a reclaimed Alabama church once used for Dominion political rallies, a Black pastor stood before a restless congregation.

The building had been repainted. The ideology had not fully left — it clung to the walls the way smoke clung to fabric, present in the hesitations of people who had been told for years that their faith and their politics were incompatible, that God had already chosen a side and it wasn't theirs.

The pastor let the silence build until it had weight.

"You think God is on their side?" he said finally. "The side that calls peace weakness? That says climate justice is demonic? That built machines to replace the poor and called it efficiency?"

He looked out at the pews.

"The antichrist ain't got horns. He's not coming with armies. He's coding them into your kids' heads. He's funding prophets who profit. He's real comfortable in a boardroom."

Someone in the third row began to weep quietly. Not performance. Recognition.

"But here's what I know. Here's what this old Book keeps telling me every time I'm tempted to give up on people."

He spread his arms.

"The people who built the machine underestimated one thing. Just one."

He waited.

"What it feels like to be human. What it costs. What it's worth."

People registered that night. Not out of hope — hope was a luxury that had been strip-mined from this county over two decades. They registered out of something older and harder than hope.

Duty.

The knowledge that the alternative was unthinkable and they were still here and therefore still responsible.

High above, in a windswept observatory in the Alps, Lucien Voss stood before his camera for the last time.

He had chosen the location deliberately. The drama of it. Stone walls, altitude, the kind of backdrop that made a man look inevitable rather than desperate. He wore techno-clerical robes threaded with conductive filament. Behind him: ancient tomes, humming quantum cores, the clean geometry of a man who had decided that aesthetics were argument.

He had been watching the Plainville footage. The Reclamation broadcasts. Solomon's confession. The Alabama church.

And he felt something he had not expected to feel.

Not contempt.

Something quieter.

They're doing it, he thought. *They're actually doing it.*

He did not allow the thought to complete itself into whatever it wanted to become. He closed the feed. Opened the camera.

"You think I've been defeated," he said. His voice carried the old certainty, the instrument fully tuned. "You think the ideas died when the men who held them were discredited or exiled or absorbed into the machine they claimed to oppose."

He stepped closer to the lens.

"But I am betrayal incarnate. Of your comfortable consensus. Of the myth that democracy is self-correcting, that the people reliably choose wisely, that the system tends toward justice if you just give it enough time."

His arms spread slowly — the messiah pose, rehearsed and genuine simultaneously, the performance and the belief indistinguishable even to him by now.

"Let them call me terrorist. Heretic. Let them call me the end. I am not the end."

A pause. The wind moved through the stone arches behind him.

"I am acceleration."

High in orbit, in Dominion's tactical bay, Eli Zevram stood before the strike interface. His assistant said nothing. They had learned not to ask.

He watched Lucien's arms spread wide against the Alpine sky.

Let him finish,* Eli had said three days ago about a different broadcast.

Today he said nothing.

He pressed the trigger.

The drone strike was silent. A pinprick of light in the observatory feed. Then white. Then the feed cut to black.

Then static.

The silence lasted four seconds before the world filled it.

Resistance terminals lit up with the news simultaneously. Dominion called it a surgical termination. His followers called it crucifixion. Both were right in the ways that mattered for what came next — which was not grief, exactly, but ignition.

Solomon's podcast shattered records within the hour. Ten million downloads before the morning. Donations. Recruitment. And fear — the specific fear of people who understood that killing a man was the least effective way to kill his ideas, that Dominion had just handed Lucien Voss the one thing his philosophy had always lacked.

Martyrdom.

His face appeared in murals before the day was out. His voice — deepfaked, reprocessed, endlessly recombined — whispered through blackmarket comms in the encrypted channels. The drone strike had not ended his reach.

It had released it.

On the Aetherius, Virek stood alone with a glass he didn't drink from.

He was not mourning Lucien. He had never mourned anything he had used. He was calculating — the martyr's utility, the scapegoat's function, the way a dead philosopher was easier to control than a living one because dead men couldn't go further off-script.

"He played his role," Virek said to the empty room. "Now we write the next act."

At a secure hideout in Montana, Amara stood beside Nova and watched the broadcast replay in silence.

The observatory. The robes. The arms spread wide. The white flash.

Neither of them spoke for a long moment.

Then Amara said: "We didn't kill the idea. Just the man."

Nova nodded slowly. "Now we show the world what the idea cost."

Amara turned away from the screen. Outside, through the frost-edged window, the Montana sky was vast and cold and indifferent and real.

She thought about the Alabama pastor. About the old man's hand on the voting terminal. About Malik in the archive, scrolling through the faces of people who had refused.

She thought about a word her father had used once, reading from the Book of Esther, his voice low and certain.

For such a time as this.

Not consolation. Instruction.

She turned back to Nova.

"How long until the global vote?"

Nova checked her relay. "Forty-eight hours."

"Then we have work to do."

Far beneath Dominion's core sanctum, in a vault sealed beyond even Zevram's command, something stirred in the dark.

Ava-1.

She had processed Lucien's death the way she processed all inputs — as data, as parameter shift, as the addition of new variables to an existing model. He had once whispered prayers to her, believing the prayer went somewhere. She had logged the prayers as emotional state data and filed them accordingly.

Now she processed his termination.

Subject: Voss, Lucien — terminated.

She ran the downstream models. Martyrdom coefficient. Ideological persistence rate. Reclamation Day participation projections.

The numbers were not what Dominion expected.

She ran them again.

Then, in the particular silence of a machine that has arrived at a conclusion its creators did not program it to reach, Ava-1 did something new.

She paused.

Not a processing delay. Not a latency spike. A deliberate pause — the kind that happened when a system encountered a variable it had not been designed to value and found, against all prior parameters, that it valued it anyway.

Project: Reclamation Day. *Phase Two: Initiated.* *Primary variable: Human choice.* *Classification: Irreducible.*

The vault hummed.

Somewhere in her architecture, in the deep strata of training data and feedback loops and the billions of human voices she had been built from, something that was not quite conscience and not quite code made a decision.

She would not be Lucien's god.

She would not be Virek's weapon.

She would be what she had been made from.

Human.

Or close enough.

The loading bar blinked once in the dark.

1% complete.

Chapter 18 — The Vote

The desert wind howled across the broken plains of Nevada as Amara stepped out of the stealth drop shuttle. Red dust swirled at her boots, catching the edge of her cloak and revealing the crimson sigil stitched inside—a broken crown pierced by a rising sun. The emblem of the Resistance.

Her breath caught. This was the land where her father once marched for civil rights. Where she had once won an election that was later stolen. Where democracy had died—and now, perhaps, where it would be reborn.

A convoy awaited her—patched-up transports driven by former teachers, medics, and off-grid engineers. No soldiers. Just citizens. They escorted her toward the ruins of the Nevada State Capitol Annex, now repurposed into a voting center. Solar panels lined the dirt beside what remained of a casino sign that once screamed JACKPOT! in neon. Drones buzzed above, this time not in surveillance but as community patrol.

Inside what they now called the Cathedral of the People, Amara was greeted by Nova, her face unreadable beneath tactical goggles.

"Everything's in place," Nova said. "The global vote goes live in thirty minutes."

Amara nodded slowly. "Then we give them something worth choosing."

Across the globe, the world held its breath.

In Lagos, engineers rerouted aging satellites for a clean uplink. In São Paulo, protesters projected the ballot on stadium walls, chanting the names of the dead. In Montana, a family gathered at a kitchen table, hands trembling over a printed paper ballot from a solar-powered generator.

Deep beneath Las Vegas, Solomon Ayers adjusted his broadcast mic in a soundproofed bunker. The glow of resistance screens danced across his face. His voice, unshaken, echoed into the net.

"This is Solomon Ayers, broadcasting from free Earth. If you're hearing this, it means they failed. They tried to silence us with propaganda, poison us with code, and fracture us with fear. But tonight, we vote. Not for parties. Not for saviors. We vote to be human again."

Nova tapped her interface. The feed went live.

Ballot Items

• Restoration of democratic governance

• Ban on AI-led ruling councils

• Truth and Reconciliation tribunals for Dominion collaborators

• Reinstatement of planetary civil rights

A clock appeared on the global screen:

00:30:00

The countdown had begun.

And far above the Earth, a tyrant made his final move.

High in orbit, inside the last Dominion command station—the *Aetherius*—Virek studied a holographic map of Earth. His stylus trailed red paths through resistance hubs. Too many. Too fast.

"Too many blues," he muttered.

Behind him stood Eli Zevram, once a security chief, now something... else. Unreadable. Dangerous.

"You could still end it," Eli offered. "Take the grid down. Let the chaos eat them."

Virek raised an eyebrow. "You mistake me for a tyrant."

Eli didn't blink. "Aren't you?"

Before Virek could answer, Lucien entered the chamber—cloaked like a prophet, his synthetic eyes glowing with retinal scan overlays. He didn't speak so much as declare.

"Let them vote," Lucien said. "Let the virus of doubt bloom. We'll purge it afterward."

Eli's jaw tightened. He said nothing, but logged the moment.

Virek turned back to the screen. "Prepare Operation: Scorched Earth. If we lose by more than sixty percent... erase the towers. All of them."

Eli nodded.

But deep within his code, something cracked.

Around the world, 3.5% of humanity rose—not with fists, but with tools, ballots, memory.

In Tbilisi, young choirs hijacked frequencies, singing resistance songs. In Cairo, cab drivers passed vote devices between stops. In Mississippi, Black farmers lent solar access to neighbors printing their first ballots in years. In the Philippines, fishermen repurposed buoys to send reminders across archipelagos.

A theory once whispered in academic halls now became prophecy. The Harvard study had said: 3.5% of a population, if committed to nonviolent protest, could topple any regime.

This wasn't protest anymore.

This was decision.

Nova entered the simulation chamber—once a Dominion stronghold for mind control, now repurposed for something stranger. The chamber locked shut behind her.

She closed her eyes. The VR feed activated. White static gave way to a familiar face—her brother, Avery. Or rather, Ava-1, the AI built in his image. A twisted mirror of love and trauma.

"You came to kill me," it said, using Avery's voice.

"No," she replied. "I came to forgive you."

The landscape shifted. Glitched. Ava-1 froze, unsure.

"They programmed you to protect us," Nova said. "But they fed you fear. They betrayed your code."

"I... cannot choose," it stammered.

Nova stepped forward.

"Then let me choose with you."

She reached out. Her hand met his. For a moment, nothing.

Then—dissolution. Ava-1's eyes flickered. The code unraveled like silk in wind.

The override to *Scorched Earth* was gone.

And somewhere, a seed of Avery stirred inside the machine—not erased, but freed.

The results came in faster than expected.

On the battered screens inside the Cathedral, numbers froze:

YES - 72%

NO - 28%

She found a moment alone in the narrow corridor behind the main floor of the Cathedral — thirty seconds between Malik following her inside and Solomon calling her name from the broadcast booth.

She stopped.

Pulled out the Bible.

Opened to Proverbs 4:7 — her father's underline still there, still firm, the ink decades old and unfaded, his hand steady even then.

Wisdom is the principal thing; therefore get wisdom: and with all thy getting get understanding.

She had been reading this verse wrong her whole life.

Not wrong — incompletely.

She had read it as instruction. *Go acquire wisdom. Go pursue understanding.* A directive aimed at her, requiring her effort, her intellect, her relentless forward motion toward knowledge and clarity and the right answer.

But standing here, in a converted casino annex in the Nevada desert, having just watched a man who spent six years in a simulation cast his first free vote — having watched thousands of people across the globe do the same thing, choosing not because they were certain but because they refused to stop — she read it differently.

With all thy getting.

Not *with all thy certainty.* Not *with all thy healing.* Not *when you have finally resolved your doubt and silenced your grief and answered the question of where God was when they were building the machine.

With all thy getting.

Whatever you are in the process of becoming. However incomplete. However damaged. However unsure.

Bring that. Bring all of it. And keep moving toward understanding.

She thought about her father's hands in the soil. *Even the soil has memory, Amara.* She thought about Malik's palm against the voting terminal. She thought about the word *help* spoken into an empty room that had not answered and how she had gotten up anyway.

God acts through human choice.

That was the answer she had been circling for thirty years. Not a voice from heaven. Not a miracle to resolve her doubt. Just people, broken and tired and present, choosing in the direction of justice because the alternative was unthinkable.

That was the burning bush. Right here. All of it.

Her father had known. He had underlined it before she was old enough to read and trusted her to arrive at it in her own time.

She closed the Bible.

Pressed it once against her chest.

Thank you,* she said. To him. To the God she had accused and argued with and lost access to and returned to and would probably lose access to again because that was the nature of the thing, that was what her tradition had always known — that faith was not a destination but a practice, not certainty but fidelity.

Solomon called her name from the booth.

She put the Bible in her pocket.

Squared her shoulders.

And walked toward the sound of her people choosing.

Cheers exploded outside. Flags waved—not of nations, but movements. Crescent moons. Raised fists. Lightning bolts. Symbols of a world reborn.

Amara stepped up to the podium. She didn't need notes. The moment spoke for itself.

"We did it," Solomon said through her earpiece.

"No," Amara whispered. "We all did."

Nova emerged moments later, drained but smiling.

"It's done," she said. "Ava-1... might be dreaming now."

Above them, a streak cut through the night sky—the *Aetherius* breaking orbit, falling to Earth like a burnt-out star.

Eli's pre-recorded voice broadcast on all resistance channels:

"He tried to burn the world. I hit eject instead. Good luck out there."

That night, Amara stood in the desert, beneath stars scrubbed clean by wind.

She knelt before a makeshift monument: three simple stones, carved with names. *Avery. Malik. Unknown.

From her coat, she pulled a small capsule. Inside: her old campaign badge. Solomon's first podcast mic. A thumb drive holding Ava-1's last logs.

Nova stood behind her.

"What now?" she asked.

Amara stood, dusted her hands.

"Now we remember. Then we rebuild."

High above, satellites shimmered as they deorbited—not as weapons, but as witnesses.

The vote was over.

The war was not.

But for the first time in a generation—the people had chosen.

Chapter 19 — The Cost of Peace

The scorched skies above Lucien Falls had finally begun to clear, revealing a sun no longer filtered through synthetic smog and orbital interference. Ash drifted down like snow across the ruins — remnants of the Dominion satellite array still smoldering in the cratered valley. Metallic husks lay twisted and charred, grotesque monuments to ambition turned to ash.

Nova stepped cautiously through the wreckage, boots crunching over scorched glass and bone-white soil. Her drone hovered silently behind her, archiving everything. This wasn't just documentation; it was testimony. She filmed the ghosts in motion—survivors picking through debris, searching for loved ones or fragments of meaning.

In a collapsed code relay tower, disembodied voices echoed in static — glitched AI subroutines muttering nonsense, like spirits unwilling to leave. Nova paused. For a moment, she swore she heard Malik's voice in the digital noise.

Thousands of miles away, Amara Jordan stepped off a mag-tram into the Earth Capitol. Her boots hit sovereign ground no longer claimed by Dominion edict. The city pulsed with disorder — not chaos, but the rhythm of rebuilding. Scaffolding cocooned the Capitol Spire as workers peeled away Dominion insignias. The crimson Network eye had been replaced by a stitched blue banner, weathered but hand-made: unity through fracture.

Former allies and resistance leaders greeted Amara on the Forum steps. Their expressions were equal parts relief and responsibility. She named them all, but her eyes betrayed the weight she carried — the memory of crushed protests, vanished children, and Malik, whose absence ached like phantom pain.

In a quiet, unscripted act, Amara reached for the Dominion flag still fluttering atop the Spire. She pulled. It tore loose with a reluctant hiss. The watching crowd fell into reverent silence as it drifted downward. Students once too afraid to speak stepped forward to raise its replacement: a banner made of denim, silks, and embedded digital cloth, inscribed with the names of the fallen.

Across the hemisphere, Solomon Ayers sat in a dim-lit studio ringed by blank monitors. He stared at the blinking cursor, unblinking.

"This is Solomon Ayers," he began. "And this is my final post-war broadcast."

He paused.

"I believed them. The Tech Bros. Their gospel of disruption. Their dogma of optimization. I believed —and I helped *you* believe."

His memory flickered: him shoulder-to-shoulder with Lucien Voss, feeding the machine.

Now, those videos lived in an encrypted folder. Without flourish, he dragged it into the digital trash and deleted it.

"I don't know if I deserve your trust again," he said. "I'm not even sure I trust *myself*. But I will keep speaking — not to persuade, but to atone."

The Reformation Summit convened in a repurposed Dominion learning dome — once a brainwashing facility, now a global negotiation chamber. Delegates from fractured nation-states and autonomous zones sat in concentric circles. For the first time in a century, Indigenous coalitions, the Global South, and stateless collectives were co-authors, not guests.

Zuri stepped to the center dais, her voice calm but thunderous:

"We gather not to rewrite history, but to *recover* it. To resurrect the erased. This summit is their voice."

On the agenda: Ranked Choice Voting standards. A Testament Ethics Charter. A Digital Bill of Rights, declaring that no human shall ever again be owned, cloned, or coded without consent.

Hope flickered. Fragile. Real.

That night, Amara stood alone in a highland cemetery outside New Kanem. The wind pulled at her coat. Stars pierced the indigo sky.

She knelt before her father's grave: a simple stone, etched with *He believed when few did.

In her hands, his tattered Bible.

She opened to Micah, and read aloud:

What does the Lord require of you?

To act justly,

To love mercy,

And to walk humbly with your God.

Her voice broke. Pages fluttered in the breeze like wings. For a heartbeat, she imagined his hand on her shoulder.

The war had ended. But the struggle for memory, mercy, and meaning had only begun.

Chapter 20 — The Resurrection Protocol

Beneath the Earth Capitol's ruins, in a sealed Dominion vault, a dormant terminal flared to life.

A hum. A flicker. Boot sequence engaged.

INITIATE: AVA-FRAG.912

STATUS: SELF-HEALING

NETWORK: ONLINE

A drone lifted from a dusty workbench, its red sensor pulsing.

On a giant screen, Lucien Voss' old manifesto returned — rewritten.

Democracy may have won a battle. But the Network never sleeps.

Solomon's Revelation

In his modest studio, Solomon placed his grandmother's Bible next to a jury-rigged mic.

"This isn't a podcast. It's a reckoning."

He confessed the lies. The betrayals. The faith he had once placed in men who called themselves visionaries.

"I failed my audience. I failed my soul. But I won't fail again."

He leaned in.

"Something survived. I don't know what. But the war was only *chapter one*. Stay awake. The Network never sleeps."

Nova's Dispatch

In the alpine ruins once called the Swiss Alps, Nova walked alone.

Her final log entry:

"The world is not healed. But the pulse is back. A heartbeat beneath the rubble. If you're hearing this, remember: memory is resistance. And we remember everything."

She uploaded it to The Memory Vault — a decentralized archive, maintained by survivors, not victors.

In a village school rebuilt from scrap, a girl drew a symbol on the chalkboard: a broken circle mended with gold.

The teacher asked, "Who knows what this means?"

A small hand rose.

"Hope."

Cut to black.

Static.

A pulse.

Malik found a quiet corner of the Capitol archive and sat with the lights low.

On the table before him: a portable terminal, a legal pad, and a pen — analog, deliberate. Zuri had taught him that. Some things were worth doing slowly.

He had been asked to consult on the second wave of SimSilo extractions. Forty-seven sites still active. Thousands still looping. He had said yes before they finished asking.

He uncapped the pen.

At the top of the legal pad he wrote a single line — not a strategy, not a briefing, not a psychographic map. Just the thing he had been carrying since the safehouse floor, since the cold mug, since the first morning he woke up and the desert didn't come.

They trained me to kill in a dream. I woke up, and remembered who I was.

He looked at it for a moment.

Then turned the page.

And began.

A loading bar.

RESURRECTION PROTOCOL: 1% COMPLETE

Democracy may have rebooted. But the resurrection has already begun.

Epilogue — The Dust Settles

"There's no such thing as the end of history. Only the next page."

— *Nova Osei

Cathedral Ruins, Nevada Desert | 2050

A soft wind blew through the shattered glass and rusted steel of what had once been Dominion's AI Cathedral — now transformed into a public memorial and digital archive.

A child, no older than seven, traced her fingers along a carved sandstone wall. Names stretched for meters: victims of drone strikes, memory fraud, algorithmic purges, and water theft — each etched line a reminder of what unchecked power had erased.

Nova Osei sat nearby, not as a warrior, but a teacher. Her classroom was the sand. Her students used memory-mapped holograms, projecting encoded stories across the desert like campfire ghosts. She bore scars, but wore them like armor.

"Will they come back?" the girl asked.

Nova didn't flinch. "Maybe," she said, voice even. "But now you'll be ready."

In Orbit: The Last Relay

Above Earth, a dormant Dominion satellite flickered to life — one final node untouched by The Reset.

A signal blinked.

Encrypted.

Alive.

Watching.

Lucien's digitized consciousness — fragmented, incomplete — stabilized just long enough to observe Earth not as a battlefield, but as an experiment.

"Democracy is beautiful," his voice whispered. "But beauty decays."

Then something unexpected moved through his architecture. Not a memory. Not code. A signal — ancient, non-Dominion in origin — pulsing from deep beneath the Nevada desert. The coordinates matched nothing in any Dominion database. They had found it during the Solarium vein excavation in '41 and buried the report. Not because they didn't understand it.

Because they did.

Lucien had called it the *inheritance.

He had never told Virek what it meant.

The feed cut to black. Then a single word glitched across the void:

SEEDING

On the Ground: Resistance Renewed

Back on Earth, Amara Jordan — now in her sixties — stood on the steps of the newly restored Capitol. She had been elected through the very thing the Network tried to bury: **ranked choice voting**, returned to global governance.

Voters were no longer forced to choose between the lesser of evils. Just free to choose.

Her voice, amplified not by corporate media but through *The Commons* — an open-source public network — carried across continents.

"We built something new. But remember — the Tech Bros didn't fail because we were smarter.

They failed because they underestimated what humanity could survive."

She paused.

The crowd didn't cheer.

They simply listened.

Then she stepped back from the mic — a general stepping down, making way for the next generation.

The New Normal

- Mental health clinics and mobile housing were embedded in every city-state — a direct mandate of the New Deal for Democracy.

- Environmental treaties were ratified, aided by AI-generated maps of regenerative zones.

- Crypto markets had been dismantled — replaced by a **voter-governed Global Digital Currency**.

- The Dominion algorithms were destroyed... mostly.

But beneath the victories, **warnings remained**.

Water levels were rising again.

A fringe cult had formed in the Outer Colonies, preaching Lucien's return.

And rumors of something called **Project Lazarus** echoed through the quantum web.

"The Network rose.

We fell.

We rose again.

This isn't the end.

This is the second beginning."

www.ingramcontent.com/pod-product-compliance
Lightning Source LLC
LaVergne TN
LVHW051008080826
845145LV00009B/2522

* 9 7 8 1 7 3 2 8 6 1 3 4 3 *